PIPE DREAM

PIPE
Dream

KL COLLINS

WordCrafts

Pipe Dream is a work of fiction. All References to persons, places or events are fictitious or used fictitiously.

Pipe Dream
Copyright © 2017
KL Collins

Cover concept and design by David Warren.
Edited by Ansley Blackstock

Published by WordCrafts Press
Buffalo, Wyoming 82834
www.wordcrafts.net

FOR MY MOM

You not only inspired me to write, but without your idea this book would never exist.

1995

CHAPTER 1

My mother was very young when I was born. She was even younger when my sister was conceived. At seventeen, my sister, Laura, was born to Sara and Paul Blackwell. My mother loved *Little House on the Prairie* and easily decided on a name for her newborn baby girl. A year later, she once again loved a part of entertainment history, and perfectly timed, another baby girl was born.

The reason behind my name is easily explained as well. I am Annie for the simple fact that Sara loved the musical with the same title.

For many years I envied my sister. Her namesake had cute pigtails and wore fun clothes. Annie was an orphan, had curly red hair and one nice dress. I guess I should just be glad I wasn't a boy or I'd have been Sandy, or worse, Daddy Warbucks.

My parents had a whirlwind relationship. They fell in love and were married in high school and had babies before they were out of their teens. They were in love and had the beginnings of a perfect recipe for a long marriage. It was missing one important ingredient though – dedication.

At twenty, my dad decided the small-town life wasn't good enough for him and left his young family behind in Virginia. He said he wanted to go into politics, the military or maybe it was acting. I'm not sure now, and it didn't matter then. He chose to leave us and that is all I remember.

When I was twelve I received devastating news. My mom, sister, and I were going to live with my grandma and grandpa in Pennsylvania. Even more devastating was when I overheard my grandma talking with my mother about the aggressive form of cancer that she was diagnosed with and the few months she had left. It hurt nonetheless when my mom finally sat us down to tell us the news. That same year we buried her. We also heard our father was living near Houston. He never came to the funeral.

Laura was the cheerleading captain, and just like fairy tales read, followed the path to happiness and fell in love with the prince, the star quarterback of the high school. Upon graduation he was recruited by the Navy and married my sister. The perfect life for the perfect couple. I, on the other hand, didn't have a knight in shining armor waiting in the wings to sweep me off my feet after receiving my diploma.

My grades were simply average, and I didn't even have a penny saved to help send me to school. So instead of college I proudly poured hard work into each paycheck. I enjoyed living in my own apartment, even if it's located directly above Joey's – the only watering hole in town. It is here that I also work.

Having just turned twenty-one the last place you'd want to find yourself working is in a bar. But that was exactly where I was, and as I filled the dishes with pretzels I sighed, thinking that with all the reminiscing I'd rather be drinking at the bar than working behind it.

Joey Cantrell is my boss and landlord. I watched him curiously as he now talked on the phone. He seemed excited but nervous. Clicking the pen is a bad habit he has when nerves got the better of him. He wrote frantically and agreed repeatedly with the caller. "They will be ready. Yes, four of them...they are all vacant", he replied through the phone to an unheard question. He then hung up.

"Am I getting new neighbors?" I asked.

Without looking up from his notepad he quickly replied, "Yes, but only for a few weeks, couple months at most."

I wiped the crumbs from the counter and set out the clean ash trays trying to understand the response I just heard. I turned around, but before I could ask questions I realized Joey was gone. The clock offered a glaring reminder. I had less than ten minutes before we opened for business, and the mystery at hand would need to wait until later.

Mickey's our best customer, or at least that is a self-proclaimed title he liked to shout each night when he walks in. Tonight was no exception. "Your number one customer has just arrived!" he bellowed as he slid into 'his seat' at the far left side of the bar.

Mickey's also the town gossip. He would probably talk about himself if he could, but it is rumored he is worse than Shirley Johnson, the beauty salon owner out on Vine street. A customer waiting in Shirley's salon would find herself very limited in the variety of magazines to choose from. She only subscribed to those that featured celebrity gossip.

So it's no exception that when Mickey entered he came armed with fresh news off the street. "Guess what's coming to town?"

I took a deep breath, furrowed my eyebrows, and slowly blew out my breath. After a dramatic ten-second wait I answered, "The circus... carnival...Santa...no, wait, it must be the President of the United States. I'm right, aren't I?"

He chuckled his deep, sincere laugh while he shook his head. "Nah... Nothin' that exciting. Pipeline's coming through town though... Sure they'll be tearing up the fields along the highway and causin' traffic jams. Good thing it's only for a few weeks."

As soon as he said a few weeks the brief conversation with Joey came back. It made sense now. He was offering the vacant apartments to the pipeline company.

For the next two hours Mickey expanded on the news he shared. He talked about the conversations he overheard at the gas station and the article in the paper detailing the timeline of the work that was to be completed. With two separate crews the entire job would be done within two to three months. The first crew was to arrive within a few days. I understood now why Joey was so nervous about getting everything in order.

This thought gave me an idea. It was Friday, and besides working Saturday night I was scheduled off that weekend. I picked up the phone and called Joey's house. I left a message explaining that with my free time that weekend I would like to help him get ready for the workers. I knew there were last minute repairs and cleaning that needed to be done.

I watched Mickey as he continued to talk, and as the evening progressed each unsuspecting customer who sat near him got roped into a deep conversation on a controversy regarding the possible closure of the local pharmacy and how the loss of business would have the domino effect on the other locally owned establishments.

I couldn't help but laugh at the latest gentleman who sat beside him now carefully eyed the room for the closest exit to escape. I wandered over in their direction to offer such relief as Mickey got distracted with my attention.

Every stool was full and the place was packed. It was standing room only and another busy Friday was flying by. Drinks were made and bottles were opened as fast my fingers would work. Around eleven the crowd thinned and I found myself able to finally take a break. I sat down on the stool Mickey vacated two hours before and took the list of items Joey said needed to be done in the apartments. Not bad, especially since the apartments were just sitting vacant. The extra two hundred dollars he offered for my help would be nice as well. My savings account would thank me.

CHAPTER 2

Monday morning the town began to change. The pipeline company had arrived. Trucks and equipment rumbled down Main Street, and like a parade, the people milling in the area stopped mid-stride and turned to watch the procession make its way across town. I stood on my balcony overlooking the west side of the street and took a long sip on my coffee. I was engrossed just like everyone else. This was indeed big news for the community.

Someone frantically knocked on my door, and my coffee splashed down the front of my track suit. I dabbed myself with a towel and answered to find Joey out of breath and sweating.

"They're here," he said, breathlessly.

"Calm down, everything you needed done has been taken care of. I finished your list and then some, and the keys for the apartments are in an envelope by the register. Now, breathe... you want some coffee?"

He panted, nodding his head.

I poured a cup and added cream and sugar as I know he liked. "If there are at least twenty loads of trucks coming through town where is everyone staying?"

He moved to the table. "From what I understand, most of those staying here are supervisors and senior apprentices; the rest of the crew will be in the extend-a-stay motel out by Finley."

"And for how long is that?" I hated change, and especially when the unknown came with it. I didn't know these guys, didn't trust them, and certainly didn't know what to expect. It was apparent in my question.

He laughed through a swallow, almost choking on his coffee. "Don't worry, I told your grandpa I'd watch out for you... but just to be safe you'd better lock your door… wouldn't want anyone to walk in your apartment by mistake after a night in the bar."

I threw my towel at him. "Not funny." Joey and my grandfather worked in the same factory many years ago. They shared lockers and stood beside each other on the assembly line. When the plant shut down they remained friends even after they moved in different directions. My grandfather became a shift supervisor for another factory in the next town over, and Joey opened the bar.

Growing up he has been the dad I never had. He has protected me, guided me, and been there with a shoulder to cry on when I was upset. He even offered an apartment for a very reduced price for me when I graduated high school. I know I wouldn't have to worry about the pipeline workers, or even the boogie man if he was around, and this was another reason I still worked for him today.

CHAPTER 3

From the first day the workers were in town every business in town miraculously grew. The barbershop took in new clients for haircuts, the diner was full for each meal, and the stores' registers collected more money than any Christmas holiday season's ever seen. The bar was no exception this Monday night. Usually during the week the regulars would show on their favorite days, but the stools along the bar were never full. Tonight they were.

Rugged, dirty men laughed jovially with each other and shared stories of the road and families back home. Their rough beards were covered in foam from the beer, and in cases where some men showered their "good" shirts resembled something I'd just cleaned their rooms with that past weekend.

"Only for a few weeks," I mumbled under my breath.

During the week Joey's closed at midnight. It's very rare though that any customers are left after eleven o'clock. As I finally got the opportunity to start cleaning the bar I glanced at the wall clock behind me.

It was ten till midnight. No wonder I was exhausted.

There were two men that remained at the far right side of the bar. One stood up throwing a few dollars on the bar, turned, and left. The other one, younger of the two, took the last long drag of his beer and set the bottle loudly down, the thud echoed around the empty room.

"I'm sorry but we're closing in ten minutes." I nodded in his direction. "I'll have to cash you out now."

He pulled out his wallet, "How much do I owe you?"

I glanced at the receipt, "twelve dollars and fifty cents."

Without saying a word he threw down a twenty dollar bill and

9

stood up to leave. He grabbed his worn yellow baseball cap and jammed it down over his red curls.

The motion seemed to have been done in anger. I wasn't sure why, and it honestly didn't matter. I just wanted desperately to leave. My feet were tired. My mind was even more exhausted.

"Hey!" he yelled with one hand on the door.

I turned to see why he was yelling and saw him staring at me.

"What's your name?" he asked.

I stood there debating whether I should throw out a fake one but thought better of it since he was sure to come back and hear otherwise. "Annie," I yelled back.

Without acknowledging that he even heard me he was gone, but not before I distinctly saw him repeat my name under his breath.

CHAPTER 4

That next afternoon I was more prepared for the new crowd. I set out extra bowls of snacks and made sure the cooler was well stocked with the most popular longnecks from the night before.

Laughter vibrated around the room again, and I began to make small talk with some of the new guests. I learned where each of them stayed in the apartments, and even began to remember names. Josh and Phil were cousins, and Billy was their uncle by marriage. They were all rooming together. Scotty was a widower, and AJ just graduated high school. I learned that Vince was a father of four boys and shared the apartment beside me with Will, the hopeful songwriter from Nashville. They promised to keep a watch over my place when possible.

I laughed wondering where they've been for the last three years that I've lived on my own. Pete was the oldest and had been with the pipeline the longest. He was a divorced man married to his work now.

From talking with newest customers, those with the pipeline, I learned that some stories were interesting, sad, and funny to say the least; but I most wanted to know about the redhead sitting with an older man with leathered dark skin, an obvious pipe worker aged by the constant sunshine and who I assumed was Paul. Once in a while I would catch the redhead glance my way. Eventually his partner left for the night, and he moved to his same seat at the far side of the bar.

I made my way toward him. "Hey there."

He nodded. "Annie, how are you this fine evening?" He was relatively pleasant sounding, but sarcasm dripped off the question.

I took away the empty glass in front of him. "Tired." I forced a smile. "How about yourself?"

He sighed. "Good, considering all this." He waved a wide arch around him.

I didn't want to ask what the gesture meant. He didn't seem much into small talk tonight, and remembering last night's quick exit, possible ever. I slowly moved away and continued to clean. The evening had turned to night, and even though most customers had cashed out there was still a tremendous mess left behind.

I was loading dishes into the sink at the other end of the bar. Mickey was in his usual spot telling a tale of the latest affair he heard about while pumping gas in town. "The sun will come tomorrow, bet your bottom dollar that tomorrow…" someone sang, and I quickly turned around. The red headed gentleman diverted his eyes to his drink, but couldn't help look up at my reaction.

"Excuse me?" I asked.

"That is who you were named after, right? Although, she didn't have blonde straight hair. I can't image it was after Annie Oakley either, so I'm guessin' your mom just loved the musical. Am I right?" It was the most I'd heard him say to me since he was there.

"Yeah, you're right, Mister…?"

I was getting his name one way or another.

"James, just James… no Mr."

Well that was better than nothing. "So, James, why the interest in my name, and it seems to me like you've had a bad day today."

He grumbled. "Nah, not a bad day, just not exactly where I want to be."

I now stood right in front of him and really looked at him. He was young, but not young like Will, the songwriter, or AJ, the recent high school graduate, and he wasn't old like Billy, or the man I noticed him sitting with earlier. He was handsome in a rugged way but his eyes also showed something else. They were sad.

"Miss!" Another local at the bar shouted. He waved a ten-dollar bill in the air with one hand and had his arm around his laughing girlfriend with the other. "Can I get change before we leave?"

I jerked back from my trance realizing I was staring longer than the few seconds than I thought. I turned around and could feel my face grow warm with embarrassment. I quickly made the change and looked back at James. He was tossing back peanuts, but clearly there was a smile plastered on his face. He caught me.

CHAPTER 5

Wednesday morning I woke up by seven. I couldn't sleep. I put on coffee and opened the balcony door. There was a small group of pipeline workers gathered outside the bakery next door. "Mornin'," Vince bellowed, holding up his coffee giving cheers. "We didn't wake you, did we?"

"Good morning, gentlemen, and no, I just couldn't sleep," I laughed. "And I'll be even better when my coffee is done."

He walked up to the balcony and tossed a pastry bag skyward. "Here, this chocolate chip muffin will make that coffee even more perfect."

Reaching out, I caught the bag. "Yes it will, thank you!"

It smelled fresh and still felt warm. As I was telling them to have a good day I noticed the familiar yellow baseball cap walk out the door. James took a long sip off his coffee and glanced my way. He nodded once in acknowledgement and walked to the driver's side of the truck.

My phone rang making me leave my vantage point. I threw my muffin onto the counter before answering. "Hello?"

"Hey, it's Laura," my sister said, out of breath. "Sorry it's so early. I can never get the time difference right. So how is everything back home? I haven't talked to you in a while."

I filled her in on my new neighbors and how busy I was at work. She told me of the new puppy she was hoping to get soon, and how her husband's new papers were being processed, and that they might be coming back stateside very soon. For the next ten minutes we caught up with each other since the last call a week before.

I spent the rest of the morning cleaning house and doing laundry. By lunchtime I was in the mood to get away from the apartment and bar.

I debated shopping and what I needed for the apartment from the grocery store, but before I attempted the trip to the super center I needed to grab a bite to eat. The muffin from this morning had long been worked off.

As I sat in the sub shop eating lunch I began to feel sorry for myself. "Where the heck did that come from?"

I have long been an introvert, a loner of sorts and actually loved this quality about myself. I could shop for hours by myself or curl up and read a five-hundred page novel in a weekend. It has been satisfying to me, but just talking to my sister this morning gave me this tremendous sense of loneliness. She had Matt and traveled all around the world with him. And their friends numbered more than the citizens of this town. I realize my two best friends were my landlord-slash-boss and Sassy, my overweight free-spirited tabby cat.

My grandma and grandpa are still well and alive. They lived about half a mile outside of town in a picture-perfect country house, complete with a white picket fence and a bird feeder hanging from each tree. Their house and landscaping also represents my life growing up—picture perfect, yet I am not as close to them as even the man who hands me a paycheck.

I look around at the other familiar faces in the restaurant. This town is very small, and everybody eventually learns everything about everyone. Neighbors say hi when you pass them in the street, and as I quietly watch a couple of residents eat and talk, I can easily run down their life histories. I know their kids, and where they work, and the street they live on.

At twenty-one most of my friends are still in college or have found new lives outside the state. A small tear creeps down my face. Sadly, I envy both groups.

"Annie?" Sylvia, an elderly friend of my grandma had walked up behind me. "Are you ok, sweetie?"

I quickly wiped my face and snapped out of my daydream forcing a smile, "Oh yes ma'am, just finishing up my lunch."

She patted my shoulder as she walked by. "Keep your chin up, and tell your grandma hello from me when you talk to her."

Nodding, I grabbed my empty cup and tray and headed to the trash can. I no longer felt like shopping, and I certainly didn't want to run into anyone else while feeling sorry for myself, so I headed back to the bar. It would be quiet there, and I could easily find something to do.

After deep cleaning the bathrooms and reorganizing the supply closet I quickly realized the irritating sound of silence. As much as I wanted to be alone I still need company, even the nonhuman kind. I turned on the jukebox and switched the setting to continuous play and then turned the volume up. Sneezing after reaching behind the jukebox I remembered another chore, dusting. That was a definite must. I grabbed the rag and spray and danced around to an upbeat country song. Just as I began shouting the lyrics into the can I heard laughter from the doorway.

Watching me with a grin on his face was James No-Last-Name. "No, don't stop. You are a great singer." He applauded me.

I threw down the cleaning supplies and quickly pulled the jukebox plug bringing the silence back to the room. I was completely embarrassed. "What are you doing here? It's only four o'clock." It was then that I noticed rain was pounding the windows.

"Early end to the day." He continued to smile and nodded to where I was looking. "Is Mr. Cantrell around? I need to let him know the ceiling in our bathroom is leaking. "

I couldn't look him in the eye, and my face was as hot as fire. "No, he won't be here until five o'clock. I was just cleaning."

"I know. I saw." He chuckled.

I ignored him and used the cordless phone on the table nearby to call Joey. He quickly answered and said, "Let him know I'll meet them in the apartment in fifteen minutes."

James turned to leave and smiling he said, "I'll see you later Annie. Maybe we can do a duet when I come back." He quickly shut the door behind him as he left. Lucky for him, because the can of cleaner ricocheted off the doorframe as I kicked it across the room.

CHAPTER 6

The shower was good, so good, in fact, that the thought of leaving dampened my mood, and I remembered having to get ready to face James again at the bar.

But oddly enough, instead of throwing on my old clothes and forgoing makeup I found myself trying on outfits and checking my reflection in the mirror. I dried my hair and ran a curling iron through the strands to give it lift instead of piling the wet mound onto the top of my head and clipping it down. I actually wanted to look good.

But why did I care? I haven't tried to impress anyone since my prom date during my senior year. And looking back I actually wanted to catch the eye of Monica's date, Jeremy, who even if I stood in front of him naked with a blinking neon arrow pointing to my goods would still find a way to ignore me.

That was my life in high school, invisible Annie. Mostly, I wanted it that way, but I guess after graduating and watching everyone move on you can quickly realize that certain untaken opportunities might have actually made a social life a lot easier if handled differently.

I loved theater but refused to try out for the senior play for fear of what the 'cool' kids who I sat with at lunch would think. And then I also sat out cheerleading tryouts because my friends in the French club despised the dumb blondes bouncing around the field. So, I pleased everyone, but me... and Jeremy.

I laughed thinking about him. I may work at a bar and have a cat for a roommate, but my situation was far more promising than his. He had married Monica right after high school, and they had twin baby girls the following year. He never went to college with the football scholarship he was offered and now works on the second shift at the shirt factory in town. They live with Monica's parents. To make the situation more comical, he gained at least forty pounds and began to already lose his hair. I don't envy that nor do I look to impress him anymore when he wanders into Joey's. And even at my worst, he sits on the stool and tries to flirt with me. I now imagine smashing that neon arrow over his head, and that is why it was so funny to me.

As I walked out the bathroom door I stopped and opened the medicine cabinet searching for the pink bottle with the purple cube top. I sprayed myself with perfume, made a final check in the mirror, and headed downstairs to the bar. I felt a smile creep onto my lips. It had been a while since I felt so good about myself.

The rain was still pounding outside. I slammed the door behind me as I entered the bar. If it rained during the week even the regulars stayed home, so I expected the workers might be the only ones to show that evening. By six thirty there was still nobody there.

"Quiet night," Joey commented. "I think I'll head into the office for a while, but let me know if a crowd surges in here and you need help."

"Ok, will do. Everyone must be scared of the rain," I answered, grabbing the newspaper and climbing on a barstool. I was disappointed. Where was everyone?

Like an answer to my question the bell above the door jingled to life a few minutes later. A coat fashioned into a tarp covered a figure that ducked quickly inside.

"Cats and dogs don't have anything on that. It's more like cows and horses coming down out there," James said as he shook off the rain from the coat and draped it over the back of the stool. He looked around. "Are you even open?" he asked. "It's dead in here."

"I was just going to ask you where all the guys were? I began to think everyone left town." I felt the disappointment start to leave.

"Well, Billy, Josh, and Phil never miss church on Wednesday night, and everyone else is playing poker. It's been tradition to hold poker night Wednesday night to help everyone get through the rest of the week," he explained.

"What about you? Why aren't you there?"

"I'm no good at poker. Plus, I can think of better things to do."

I smiled, blushing and walked around the bar. I poured him his favorite beer into a tall mug.

He winked and drank a long swallow ending with a loud sigh of approval.

"Looks like it's just us, Little Orphan Annie."

I pretended to not hear his nickname for me but decided it would be a long night if I ignored him completely. I grabbed a glass of ice water and bowl of mixed nuts, and slid into the stool diagonally from him. That is when I noticed how ruggedly handsome his face was. His eyes were a soft blue and his cologne reminded me of a sample from a recent ad in a sports magazine I was forced to read in the dentist's waiting room last week.

He watched me scrutinize his face. "Well, looks like you want to talk so go ahead… ask what's on your mind."

I threw a handful of nuts into my mouth and slowly chewed making him wait while gathering my thoughts. I took a drink of water adding to the suspense. "I am just curious about who you are, James Doe. Tell me about yourself."

"First, my last name isn't Doe, it's Murphy." Lifting his hat he continued, "As you can tell I'm Irish, and I come from a devout Catholic family. My mom is Caroline and my dad is Michael… well stepdad, but he's all I've ever known as a dad. I have a younger brother named Eric. We had a pretty uneventful childhood growing up in Texas. My mom stays at home, my dad owns a bar outside Houston, and my brother manages a catering business.

"When I was right out of high school I learned of the pipeline, and found out that they made a lot of money. I signed up as soon as they'd take me. Then, on break one winter I got married on a whim and when she found out my job would continue to take me out of town she left me." He paused to take a drink, and I did the same, waiting for him to continue.

If he was waiting for me to be shocked I didn't let on that I was. He looked down at the glass.

"I didn't want to work the pipeline all my life, but I wasn't a talented chef like Eric. In fact, I wasn't talented in anything, so physical work was all I knew. Honestly, what I want to do the most is work with my dad or Eric, and learn to do what they do so well. One day I want to be there with my brother carrying on our father's legacy. Seems like nothing more than a pipe dream I know, but it's something I work every day toward which is more than most people do. But instead of slowing down they keep working me harder and in turn promoted me to supervisor. It's hard to want to quit that... even if it's something I really don't like to do." He suddenly stopped and looked up. "Sorry, I don't get to talk much, and when I do most people don't want to take the time to listen. Rambling on can be a bad habit. It's your turn. Talk to me."

I started from the beginning tell of my loving mom and her early marriage to my father. How my sister and I not only faced the changes of the move to Pennsylvania but also my mom's sudden diagnosis and death. He sat and listened in silence.

"I know what you mean about not wanting to waste your time working in a job that's not ideal. I want to go to college more than anything. I've been saving everything I can, and will continue to save until I get there, no matter how long I have to wait." I was embarrassed for telling my secret.

Instead of stopping, I found myself going on. "And I want to own something, more than one something I guess... a house, a car, a boat. I want it all. More than my parents ever had." I paused, thinking my mom never even had a house. We moved from an apartment to my grandparents' house. Then she was gone. How sad to just realize that fact. It took a minute to rewind to where I left off. "And I want even more, like children, and a better future for them than what I had."

James stopped me to ask a question. "Sorry, but do you know what you want to go to school for?"

"Yeah, but not as specific as I'd like," I said. "I want to be in charge."

"In charge? That's it?" He laughed.

I smiled. "Yeah, in charge--like a teacher to a classroom, or a lawyer to a courtroom, or even a business owner. Like I said before. I want more than I had growing up, more than my mom had."

"Well even though I had an ideal childhood with the picture-perfect family, I still ended up doing something that I wasn't meant to do. Don't get me wrong, I want a family, too, but it's too hard for me to start over as far as school goes. It's harder for me at thirty-two years old to go back than for you to start now." He drank the last of his beer and I stood up to get him a refill. While behind the counter I opened a jar of pickles and quietly offered one to James willing him to continue.

Instead he changed the subject. "What do you do besides dream of college?"

I realized the depth the conversation took and was glad to make the switch. "Well, as you witnessed today it's singing and dancing. My namesake would be proud."

The easy conversation continued until ten o'clock. Joey had joined in about an hour before, and the three of us laughed and learned about each other while sharing our stories. I felt that it was a good evening and fought to hide my disappointment since it was unfortunately quickly coming to a close. James said his goodbyes ten minutes later, and I had changed into pajamas and was in bed by ten thirty.

The television was on, but I didn't even know what was on the screen. I was thinking back through the evening and replaying the conversation with James from the beginning. Of course I remembered what he had said, but it wasn't the words I was thinking about, it was his mouth as he laughed, his eyes as they thought back to his past, and the way he motioned with his hands as he talked. These traits are what I didn't want to forget about tonight. They were also the last thing I thought about before falling asleep.

CHAPTER 7

Thursdays were usually a day off for me. Joey would have his nephew work the bar on those evenings, and this was the day I usually spent visiting my grandparents. I would help Gram in the garden or Pap in the garage. Whatever they needed I was there to help. When I woke up that morning I called them to get a grocery list. Today it was a small one: spaghetti, coffee, and a small bag of oranges. Even though Joey would let me borrow his car each Thursday I usually decided to take my bike. Today was no exception; especially considering the three items she needed would fit perfectly into a backpack. Gram and Pap were only three miles from where I lived, and the store was about halfway to their house. The rain yesterday had moved out and brought cooler air. It was a beautiful day for a ride.

My grandma was kneeling at the flowerbed when I rode up behind her. She was looking closely between the rose bushes and concentrating on something against the house. I knelt beside her and tilted my head to see what she was looking at. There was a baby rabbit scared and hovering in the corner. "If it wasn't so darn cute I'd be mad it. Look at what her family did to my lettuce patch." She pointed to the left. What looked like a line of bare dirt must have been where the lettuce once stood.

"Gram, get up here and give me a hug." I held out my hand to help her as I stood and took off my backpack.

She slowly got up. "So, girly, tell me what you've been up to this past week. Have the pipeline workers kept you busy at work?"

"Yes." It's all I could say. I stared off to where the bunny still hid and thought about James.

"That's it? That's the only answer to how was your week?" She asked.

"It's been good. I have been talking with someone, a new friend."

She looked at me with squinting eyes. I knew that look. She was trying to figure out what I meant. "You met a man?" she finally asked.

"Yeah, I met a lot of men this week, more than this town's seen in years. That's all that's here working on the pipeline. But I have only really talked to one," I answered.

She wrapped her arm around my waist and led me up the back steps. "Let's get some lemonade, and you can tell me all about this fellow."

As I sat at the table waiting for my lemonade I realized how much I looked forward to my Thursdays. Gram and Pap are the only family left around me. I know Laura is still my sister, but she is halfway across the world, and not available at the drop of a hat. I see Gram rub her knuckles and know her arthritis is bothering her, even though she won't say it is.

As young as my mom was when she had my sister and me, was as old as Gram was when my mom was born. Pap met Gram when he was thirty-six. She was one year younger and a nurse who just moved into town. When she was fresh out of college she married her longtime friend, and four years later he died in a mining accident. They never had children, and to get over the loss she absorbed herself in work. The hospital she worked for had closed, and she went where the next job opportunity was.

She had filled in for the factory nurse where he worked for a few weeks, and when her assignment ended Pap asked her to go to dinner. After three years of dating they finally got married. They tried to have a baby right away but weren't successful. After almost four years and giving up hope Sara was born two days before her forty second birthday.

Gram and I talked for the next three hours, and the lemonade pitcher slowly became empty. We ate lunch, snapped beans, and cleaned the kitchen together without skipping a beat. She giggled with me as I talked about James, but she warned me to not get too attached because he would be leaving soon. She didn't want to be picking pieces of my broken heart up off the floor. I laughed at the mental picture she created in my head.

And as I said my goodbyes I hugged her tight. I knew that with each hug it might be our last. I took in the smell of her shirt – lavender and arthritis cream, and then I walked up to Pap sitting in the living room watching golf on the television. I put my hand on his noting how cold it felt and knelt down to give him a hug as well. He whispered his love for me into my hair and told me his usual, 'Be careful riding that bike home' words of caution. I recited his speech along with him knowing every word that he'd say next. He was nothing if not predictable. That much was certain.

By four o'clock I was home, curled up on the couch with a tall glass of milk and cookies and just opening a crisp new romance novel when there was a soft knock on the front door. I removed a sleeping Sassy from my lap and opened the door. There stood James with a nervous smile on his face.

CHAPTER 8

Surprised. That is the only thing I felt. I was speechless. After what felt like an hour I finally asked what he needed.

"I need a favor. I was hoping you wouldn't mind going somewhere with me," he said, not showing any emotion. He carried such a quiet and reserved attitude that it made him seem almost unfriendly.

"Oh, you want me to go somewhere? Right now?" I smoothed my hands down my shirt trying to get the wrinkles out. Then I quickly ran my fingers through my hair.

"Well I need to hurry. They will be closing soon." He checked his watch. "I think I'll make it if we go now."

I glanced back at my milk and cookies, and Sassy looked up from where she was taking her nap and yawned. There certainly wasn't much I was walking away from. So, I grabbed my wallet and keys and followed him out the door not even answering his request.

At the bottom of the stairs James turned and waited for me to join him.

"I hear Carmen's is the only flower shop in town, is that right?"

"Yes. Is that where we're going?"

"Uh huh. It's down on the left, isn't it?

I had no idea what to think, but I followed his line of questioning. "That's right."

Within five minutes we opened the door to Carmen's. The owner herself was rearranging the window display.

"Hey girl! How have you been?" She gave me a hug. She curiously eyed James. "What can I get you guys?"

"That's a good question," I replied, also looking in his direction.

"Can you please give us a minute?" James quietly asked Carmen.

She moved back to the window. "Definitely! I'll be right over here when you're ready."

He walked to the cooler and looked back and forth over each arrangement taking in each type of flower, the colors, and the sizes. I looked at each one as well and after five long minutes couldn't take the suspense any longer. "Why are we here anyway?"

"I need to find a good one. It's my mom's birthday tomorrow, and I want to call something in to be delivered to her. I just don't know which one to get. I want something she'll like to look at and something that smells good too. This just isn't my thing and I thought a woman's opinion would make it easier." He never took his eyes off the flowers as he talked.

I scanned the selection again and finally pointed to one of medium size with purples, pinks and yellows. There were daises, carnations, a few roses, and beautiful large lilies. "That's the one right there. Any woman would like that. Lilies are not only beautiful and exotic, they smell fantastic too."

I stepped outside while he placed the order allowing him the privacy to make arrangements. There was a bench strategically placed in front of the flower shop. I sat and thought about what just happened in the past fifteen minutes.

I was shocked to see James at my door, more surprised to learn where we were going, and confused as to what his motive was for going there. I was nervous, anxious, excited, and scared, and finally impressed and touched to learn who the flowers were actually for. I would love to have been able to give flowers to my mom on her birthday, and I knew most sons would not even think about attempting such a gesture, especially while working out of state. That was amazing to witness.

I was deep in thought when James walked up behind me and gently touched my back. I jerked back to the moment and looked over my shoulder.

"You're right. They do smell fantastic. Thank you for your help," he said. There laying on my shoulder was a lily.

And once again, I found myself surprised.

CHAPTER 9

I usually dreaded Fridays. It was the first of two long days, and they usually ended with busy and even longer nights. Today, however, I woke up in a great mood. As much as I wanted to sleep longer I couldn't shut down my mind. I lay in bed with the covers over my head and smiled. I could barely see the sunlit trees blowing in the breeze through the shear curtains. I was in my bed cave. The temperatures were to climb in into the high ninety's today, an oddity for late June in Pennsylvania. The window air conditioner continuously blew cool air across the bed keeping me buried deep under the covers, but I kept smiling.

After we left the floral shop last evening James quickly dropped me back off at my apartment. I was taken aback by the flower, but part of me hoped he would have asked me to dinner or to go somewhere else just to spend more time with him. The other part remembered the old cut off sweats and raggedy t-shirt I had on and was anxious to get back home.

Once inside my apartment though my heart was racing. I put my flower in water and caught myself looking at it all evening. I called and left a message for Laura telling her about what happened. When I hung up I realized how much I was overreacting and remembered my Gram's advice. By the time I fell asleep I had talked myself down from the cloud I was floating on. Now, roughly eight hours later I was back in space again with my thoughts all clouded and confused.

It took a while, but I finally willed myself out of my blanket cocoon. I had a lot to do that day. I needed to talk with the admissions office at the community college about starting courses in the fall, and I needed to pinpoint a major. I had been saving up to attend college and had quite a bit in savings. I was mostly procrastinating because I didn't know what I wanted to do with my life. I aspired to be better but couldn't decide what direction that meant.

Three months ago, the college sent me a catalog the size of the Pittsburgh phonebook, and I had only started to look at it within the past few weeks. I knew time was not on my side anymore and a decision needed to be made.

Beside the catalog was an application for the scholarships and grants they offered and I needed to get it to the post office before the deadline. In order to afford a car of any kind, and the insurance, rent, tuition, and all the other bills I had, I'd need to use all the help I could find. If it meant filling out applications and following up on grant paperwork I would do it.

The issue with James would have to wait; however, knowing that I would probably see him within the next few hours did anything but ease the anxiety.

I grabbed my coffee and the catalog and sat down at the table. With a highlighter and stack of post-it notes I set out to make my decision.

Bypassing all sections telling about the school, the enrollment requirements and biographies on the professors I made it to Courses and Classes section. As I went through each letter of the alphabet I became more discouraged. Nothing stood out. There was nothing I wanted to do or felt that I would like to try.

Two cups of coffee, a bagel, and lunch later I was nearing the end of the section. Just as I was getting discouraged I stopped on one heading–Restaurant and Hotel Management. This is something I knew. I had firsthand experience with working at Joey's, and I enjoyed it. I loved working with customers and making the bar more profitable. I practically ran the place when he wasn't there. Why would I want to change directions now?

Knowing the mailman would arrive at one thirty I was holding the scholarship and grant package out the door when he arrived and had the admissions office on the phone at the same time. Thirty minutes later I was registered for fall classes and could only think of one thought. I had to tell James the good news.

CHAPTER 10

Usually, I make a casserole or large meal on Friday afternoon. It got me through the long night and then I also have leftovers for the rest of the weekend. Today I decided on baked spaghetti.

After speaking with the admissions office, I set to work on my food project. I loved being in the kitchen and even though I know I'm not the best chef I wished I could cook for more than just one. If the final creation was really big I'd take a large dish to work for Joey and anyone else brave enough to eat my cooking.

After two hours in the kitchen my eight pounds of spaghetti finally emerged from the oven. I had taken a shower and gotten ready while it was baking. I knew I only had a few minutes to spare so I ate as quickly as I could and dished out a small container for the next two days.

With potholders on each handle I carried most of the dinner out the door. One thing I've learned on my own is that leftovers may last for a few days, but I can quickly grow tired of any dish. There was no way I would ever finish that amount, and wouldn't want to anyway.

As I rounded the corner by the stairs I ran straight into Vince and Will coming in from work. They apologized and took in a big whiff from the food I was carrying.

"Yummmmy… Where are you taking my dinner?" Will asked as I passed him.

I laughed. "If you hurry you might catch some left downstairs. It's a Friday tradition I have."

Other workers standing around turned their heads and sniffed the air. It reminded me of a pack of dogs hunting fresh meat.

At the bar I noticed Joey has already pulled out plates and the few mismatched forks he'd accumulated. I called out to let him know dinner was served, and in record time he was behind the counter scooping out a helping.

"What would you do without me?" I asked.

After swallowing his first big bite he answered, "Get remarried to someone who actually likes to cook, or eat more takeout."

Within fifteen minutes the pipeline crew began arriving led by Will and Vince. Word got out about the free dinner, and you could tell they were starving. I now wished I would have made more. I should have accounted for the extra mouths, and being my newest neighbors, I certainly didn't mind offering my home cooking to them.

I became server as the line formed by the spaghetti. The next to the last person was James. He was talking to the man behind him about a problem with a piece of equipment that took most of his time that day. He absently held out his hand and took the plate not paying attention to who handed it to him or even what it was. He took a bite while still talking and stopped in mid-sentence. I watched his reaction. He opened his eyes and nodded, and after seeing me behind the counter gave a thumbs-up. "That's very good Annie. Did you make it?"

"Uh huh," I quickly replied noting how impressed he was. I handed the last man in line a plate. There was just enough left for a final small helping. Watching everyone eat, I realized that moment might have been the quietest the bar full of customers might have ever been.

CHAPTER 11

"Drink, Drink, Drink!" The crowd chanted. I made the mistake of telling Billy I'd never taken a shot of liquor. He thought it was necessary to buy me one and made it whiskey. I fought hard to not have to drink it, but when Joey joined in with the chanting I knew it was a losing battle.

Before I lost my nerve, I picked up the glass and threw back my head. Immediately my throat was on fire, then my belly burned, and I gasped for air. The room busted out in laughter, and before I knew it I was able to breathe and joined them. I didn't want to admit it was the nastiest thing I ever laid my lips on, and that was my mistake. Fifteen minutes later another one was in front of me, and the chanting began all over again.

I felt like I was on display. Everyone stared at me, and the pressure grew with every second. I shook my head and tried to divert the attention away, but the crowd wouldn't allow it. They were now screaming and cheering, and fists thumped the bar. I announced it was my last one, and in thirty minutes it would be theirs too because it was last call. I drank the shot in a much smoother gulp but again gasped at the warmth.

Immediately my mind began to fog, and I felt relaxed, hoping my legs would hold me up. The crowd seemed satisfied with the second shot and slowly began to leave. As I finished cleaning I made my way to James who pushed the shot glass of clear liquid toward me. "Now finish with this."

I shook my head. "No thank you. I have had enough for tonight."

"Do you trust me?" He looked up at me.

"You haven't given me a reason not to yet".

31

"Josh thought I needed this, but I want to share it with you. You probably poured this many times and didn't even know what it tasted like," he said.

The lime gave it away. "That's the best tequila we have."

He nodded and adjusted his baseball cap.

I stared at him debating why I shouldn't do it. We were practically closed. There was nobody left in the bar, and I didn't have to be back until that next afternoon. What the heck. I took out another shot glass and poured another one to match the one on the bar.

"Only if you do it too," I said.

"Fair enough." We toasted and took our shots at the same time.

By the time my glass landed back on the bar I knew I didn't need to take any more. The room definitely seemed to move, or maybe it was my eyes, but regardless, it wasn't the way it should have been. I had to sit down. As I pulled up the stool James stopped me. "Don't sit down just yet."

He added three quarters to the jukebox and paged through the songs. Pressing his choices into the keypad he walked back and held out his hand before the song even began.

He was so handsome, but I resisted the urge to just reach out and take it.

Annie's Song began to play. I didn't know that song was even on the jukebox. I opened my mouth but could only whisper the words. "My mother would sing that song to me." I finally gave in and accepted his invitation to dance.

Ironically, just as he took me in his arms and pulled me close Joey turned off the main lights. Whether it was perfect timing or he was encouraging romance was his secret.

Because the only light left was on the jukebox I could only see his face when he turned toward the light. I looked in his eyes for a brief second, but as I heard the lyrics of the chorus it brought back memories from fifteen years before, and I had to look away so he didn't see my face. Once again, I felt lonely even standing in someone's arms.

As the song ended James continued to hold me until I broke his hold and pulled away. I was instantly light headed. It could have been the dancing in a circle, the alcohol, the company, or all of the above. "I need to get home. I just hope I can walk there." I laughed, stumbled to the stool, and placed my hand on the seat for support.

"Let me walk you." James put his arm lightly around my shoulders. He steered me toward the door, and I locked up behind us. Within minutes we were at my front door.

"Thank you… for the dance, and for walking me home," I told him.

He nodded. "You're welcome" and backed up a step. I walked forward closing the gap once again and gave him a hug and kissed him on the cheek. His smell was intoxicating and resisting every urge a twenty-one-year-old female has I knew, I needed to get out of there immediately. I quickly said goodnight, turned and went inside my apartment. I stood with my heart pounding and back to the door knowing that if he was still on the other side he could surely hear my chest drumming against the wood.

Little did I know, he was on the other side of the door. And he was wondering the exact same thing about me.

CHAPTER 12

I didn't sleep at all that night. As much as my head was spinning from the alcohol it was also tossing around memories of dancing, wishes for more time, and hopes for another meeting soon.

By the time the sun was beginning to crest the horizon I could hardly keep my eyes open. Around six o'clock am I must have fallen asleep, and by noon I was awakened by the sound of power tools.

Peeking outside and squinting through the sunlight I saw Joey talking to a group of the workers about the broken lattice work around the deck. I quickly scanned the group and not seeing the face I was looking for lay back down and covered my head falling asleep for another hour and a half.

When I finally rolled out of bed I realized the alcohol I had the night before didn't hurt as much as I thought it would. The seven hours of sleep, although eating up most of my Saturday was exactly what prevented any hangover from sneaking up on me. I actually felt great.

I decided that I was finally going to do the shopping and errands that I missed the week before. I needed to not only get groceries but also wanted to get a haircut. From working as much as I do I usually can get by with only getting a trim twice a year, Until the next cut, I normally pulled it back in a ponytail. Although non-attractive, it was efficient and very convenient.

By two o'clock I made my way quickly through the aisles of the local superstore. I didn't use a shopping list although I knew exactly what I needed. I dodged around other customers comparing labels and searching through piles of coupons.

I could pick the cat food out with my eyes closed and knew

exactly what shelf held my favorite spaghetti sauce. I prided myself on being able to navigate through the massive store and be in line at the checkout in less than an hour. It's easy to do when you're the only person using the groceries at home.

With everything put away I sat in Natalie's chair at the hair salon just after three o'clock. She was one of the few hair stylists that didn't spend more time gossiping and catching up on a customer's life than actually cutting the hair. When we first met she told me flat out she'd rather make money and save on the chitchat. I immediately knew I had found my new hairdresser. I sat in silence as she quickly went to work. Just a few minutes and words later I paid and walked out the door.

I loved being able to do things quickly. I don't have patience and really don't like crowds. Having been in bed most of the day I was still able to get everything accomplished. It was a great feeling, and I found myself smiling and whistling as I walked home to get ready for work. I hadn't been in this good of a mood since... well, I don't know. I wonder if last night had anything, or all, to do with it.

CHAPTER 13

When I walked to the front door of the bar that evening Mickey greeted me before my hand touched the handle. He had just arrived and was ready to explode with the news that he had to share with someone.

"Guess what?" He ran up to meet me.

"Well, hello Mickey. What's new?" I answered.

"You know those guys that are always in here from the pipeline? He started his story. "Well they said they are making great time and everything should be done by fall, maybe even mid-August."

I faked my happiness. "Wow, that's great. We can get back to normal then."

"My thoughts exactly," he said.

A week ago I would have agreed with him, but a lot has happened within those few days. I needed to talk to James. I wanted to hear the update from him, and even though Mickey was rarely wrong with this gossip, I needed to hear it from someone who knew best.

The minutes of waiting turned into an hour. Many of his coworkers had already arrived and slowly Joey's was filling up. This Saturday was special because a local band was scheduled to play for a few hours. They were across the room setting up on a makeshift stage. The talking around the room got louder as the band tested the equipment.

I was also getting busier. With a band on the schedule I had help at the bar. Joey's nephew Anthony was with me, and we shuffled around each other to make drinks and wait on customers. By seven o'clock the band was playing their first song. Just as I was forgetting why I had been watching the door I was completely surprised when I heard James calling my name from the far side of the bar.

I practically ran in his direction. "Hey."

"I have something for you," he shouted, holding a brown paper bag in my direction.

I excitedly grabbed for the package and completely forgot what I wanted to discuss with him. "What is this?"

"A brown bag." He laughed.

I opened the sack and peeked inside. The smell of fried potatoes hit me before I even saw the chips. "That smells amazing," I said, reaching in to grab one. They were still warm.

"I just made them." He answered my unspoken question of where they came from.

I was impressed. Not only because he made them but because they tasted fantastic. They had a smoky barbeque flavor to them, and were as crispy as if they just came out of the hot oil.

"Just something I like to make when I'm bored." He smiled at my delight. I knew then where he had been for so long. He was making me the chips.

He smiled again as he grabbed a beer and disappeared into the crowd. I ate a handful of the chips absorbed in the wonderful taste and snapped back into reality when Anthony bumped into me as he reached for some clean glasses.

I wouldn't see James again until the band left at ten-thirty, and the crowd thinned out. When a seat came open at the bar James saddled in for conversation. I showed him the empty sack, thanked him for the chips, and asked for a refill.

"Anytime, darling," he said.

I could feel my cheeks grow red, and he quickly looked away sensing my embarrassment.

Mickey caught my attention, and at that moment I welcomed the distraction. He leaned close and whispered louder than necessary. "That band there… well I recognize the drummer from my daughter's senior class. I heard that the guy, whose name is Andy or Aaron, was once the star quarterback at the high school but failed out of class and was put on educational probation… or was it something worse involving the law?"

While he sat back and appeared to strain trying to straighten out the story in his mind or to remember to whom he heard it from I glanced back to James who was writing something down on a napkin.

"Oh, no, it was pot...that's it! I'm sure." Mickey nodded continuing his story. "And his mom was a big lawyer out at Bradberry and Huff law firm. I think she left after he was arrested. I don't think the dad is in the picture which could be why he got in trouble in the first place."

I agreed with Mickey not understanding at all what he meant and excused myself. I turned around and frowned in disappointment to see an empty stool where James was once sitting. I walked over to where he had been and saw the napkin folded with "Annie" written in small block letters.

I opened the napkin and inside was a simple note that read: "Will you do me the honor and come to dinner with me sometime next week?" I laughed at the lines he had drawn to fill in the day and time, and he wrote that he would plan the rest. He also left instructions on where to leave the note after I filled out the blank lines. Then he had simply signed a "J" at the bottom.

CHAPTER 14

As the night crawled by the note burned into my hip. I caught myself many times reaching into the pocket of my jean shorts to make sure it hadn't disappeared or changed texture. Two o'clock couldn't have come soon enough. Not only was I exhausted from the extra workload, I was anxious to get home so I could fill in the blanks on the note.

I was pathetic.

As soon as I got home I purposely avoided the note. I did everything I had to do before cleaning out my pockets. Finally, standing beside my dresser in a bra and shorts I slowly reached in and fished out the napkin.

As if it was burning my hand, I threw it on the bed. On impact it came to rest face down. I walked around the bed staring at the paper, sat beside it, and finally, after I couldn't take it any longer picked up the note, ripped it open and quickly wrote exactly what I had memorized for the past four hours. Thursday seven o'clock, I scribbled.

I searched the desk for a plain envelope. After refolding the napkin and tucking it into the envelope I sealed the letter, and before I could change my mind ran up to James' apartment and wedged it into the doorframe.

As much as I wanted to have put Sunday on the letter, since I was in the wee hours of my first day off for the week I was simply too scared, and I certainly didn't want to seem desperate. I knew he probably thought I would put that down, too. I needed time to plan, to prepare, and to get rid of the butterflies that invaded my stomach.

When I got back home Sassy met me at the door. I scooped her up into my arms giving her the much-needed attention I had unintentionally denied her over the past week. I was out of breath, and my heart thumped in my chest.

Sassy and I watched television until three-thirty in the morning. As much as I had thought I wouldn't be able to sleep I actually found myself easily drifting off to siesta land with Sassy at my side purring a lullaby in my ear.

Even more surprising, I was wide awake and sipping my coffee on my porch by ten a.m. The horizon showed that once again it was going to rain, and the wind was starting to pick up. It was changing from a cooling breeze to a warning of an impending storm.

I watched the people of town moving around quickly trying to get to where they were going before the storm came. The News 4 weather team had mentioned a very wet Sunday with one hundred percent chance of rain. Literally, when it rains here it pours.

As the rain slowly made its way across the town I was finally forced to head inside. I called Laura, but she wasn't home. I left her a long message on her machine telling her of my upcoming date with the older and rugged pipeline supervisor. I told her to call me, but no matter what she should expect a detailed follow-up call Friday.

When I hung up I immediately felt claustrophobic. The last thing I wanted to do was be stuck inside all day counting the minutes as Sunday slowly ticked by. I picked the phone back up and called Kate, my only true girlfriend in town.

She was two years older than me, had been married at twenty and was divorced by twenty-one. To deal with the pain of the break-up she found a new love, food. Not only was she shy, and obviously obsessed about her weight problem, she found a new title of shopaholic.

Because she was so quiet and reserved she rarely called to catch up, never really asked to do anything together or go anywhere, but always accepted my invitation to go to the mall. She used it as an excuse to exercise, but her credit card would say otherwise. She loved to shop, and she loved the mall.

I hated the mall. It's the dreaded necessity across town that is the hang out for teenagers, a magnet for those with rich blood, and everything I'm not. But it was a good distraction, and female companionship was one thing I realized I was starved for. A person could only take so many testosterone-filled days.

Kate was waiting at the door when I made it down the stairs to the street. I ran two steps through the rain and jumped into the car. She smiled and expressed how excited she was that I called. I then realized how truly happy I was to see her.

When we got to the mall I told her that first things were first, and I knew she wouldn't fight me on the issue, but we had to eat. The last thing I really ate was the baked spaghetti from two days ago. Nerves kept me from having an appetite but after smelling the aroma wafting from the food court my body told me I had to eat.

I chose Chinese, as I always did, while Kate went true blue American with burger and fries. As we met back at the table I started to fill her in on what was going on in my life.

"Girl, I am so happy for you," Kate said between bites. "You deserve it more than anyone I know."

I laughed. "I haven't even gone on a date with him yet."

"But you will, and it will be perfect." She seemed convinced.

We ate in silence for a few minutes and then as if a light bulb was lit I instantly saw an idea pop into her head. "You couldn't have picked a better place or company today." She smiled.

I stopped my last bite in midair. "Why?"

"You… me…. The mall… your big date… oh, let the shopping begin!"

I choked down the rice and once again laughed. She was so excited to be my personal shopper that I couldn't deny her the joy. Like a puppy knowing the shots were to come but still choosing to follow the vet to the exam room, I joined Kate in her mission.

CHAPTER 15

We walked from one store to the next. Everything I showed Kate that I liked resulted in a look of disgust, shock, or simply a shake of the head. An hour and forty minutes into the fashion extravaganza I had to take a break. I bought an iced coffee for each of us, and we found a bench by the Men's Superstore.

"You are wearing me out." I sighed.

"You need to learn to keep up with the chubby girl," she said, dragging a long drink from her straw.

I laughed and we discussed the outfits that she liked versus what I found. She called me old-fashioned, and I said she only liked the "less is more" idea.

"You're young and hot. Flaunt it, girl," Kate said.

I simply rolled my eyes. We needed to find a common ground.

As we talked I noticed the familiar baseball cap above the clothing racks in the men's store. I stopped in mid-sentence and practically dropped my drink.

"What?" Kate asked looking in the direction of my surprised eyes.

I turned around and quickly faced the opposite direction, trying to move behind the fake potted trees beside the bench.

Kate continued to watch, and when the man finally walked out from behind the rack she couldn't help but whistle. "Holy hotness. That's him, isn't it?"

I nodded with the straw plastered to my lips. I tried to look with my peripheral vision. "What's he doing?"

"Well …he's in a store at the mall…looks like he's shopping," Kate answered.

I playfully punched her. "I know that. But why?" I asked rhetorically.

Kate chuckled. "Honey, you're not the only one with a hot date on Thursday."

With that, I turned around using the tree as a shield. He was choosing dress shirts from a rack holding each one up and thoroughly examining them. I watched him looking at a red one, blue one, and finally a black one before I snapped back to reality and jumped up grabbing Kate by the sleeve. The iced coffee she was drinking spilled from the straw as she was jerked up.

"Quick, let's go before he sees us," I loudly whispered, and we headed off into the direction his back was facing.

We slipped into a small boutique, and we laughed at the irony of seeing him. I kept my eye on the door, and beside me I heard Kate gasp. I turned, and she was standing to my right holding the cutest white summer dress with tiny yellow embroidery embellishments.

"It's perfect," we both said in unison.

CHAPTER 16

Kate and I spent the next two hours continuing our trek around the mall looking for jewelry to match the newly-purchased dress. I was excited to know that James had gotten my note and was planning for our evening as well. I was anxious for Thursday to come, and my distraction was exposed when while in a party store. Kate jumped from behind a rack with a scary mask, and I showed no reaction.

She waved her hand six inches from my face, and I finally blinked and glanced in her direction taken aback by the monster looking at me. "What the…" I stopped myself.

"Welcome back to earth, princess daydreamer," Kate said removing the mask.

I was embarrassed and turned around walking toward the door. "Ok… where to next?"

We laughed down the hall, and Kate made jokes even as we got back into the car. I playfully smacked her when I sat down in the passenger seat, but the tears from laughing so hard kept falling. I loudly sighed and wiped my eyes. "This has been one of the best days I've had in a long time."

"I completely agree," Kate said, starting the engine.

When we pulled up to the apartment I invited Kate to come in for coffee and dessert, and it was apparent from her excited reaction that it wouldn't have taken much convincing for her to agree to join me.

As I threw a batch of brownies into the oven I thanked her for the good day. I had regretted not talking to her lately. I added water to the coffee maker and watched the rain finally begin to taper off outside. By the time the coffee was done the brownies were soon cooling on the stovetop.

I described who and where the workers were that were staying around me. I filled her in on every detail from the minute I first saw James to the early morning trip to his door to drop off the note. She envied my situation and as we ate the warm brownies and sipped coffee she told me about the man she had her eye on at work. Her eyes sparkled as she talked, and I wonder if that is how I looked when telling her my story about James.

We ordered pizza and continued catching up with each other over dinner. I glanced at the clock after throwing away the paper plates. It was already nine o'clock. Kate realized it too and quickly apologized for using up the remainder of my day.

"I'm so sorry," she said, practically running to the door. "You probably had so much to do on your day off, and I wasted it by talking your ear off."

"Don't apologize. I had a wonderful day. Don't be a stranger," I said as I walked her out the door.

When she left I finished cleaning up the dishes and put the leftover brownies in a container with a lid. Just as I was going to hang up the dishtowel there was a light knock on the door. I straightened the towel and looked toward the door. What did Kate forget? I glanced around the room as I walked toward the door looking for her purse, keys, anything she might have left. I couldn't see anything.

I opened the door, "Kate, what did you…"

Kate wasn't there. Instead, a white paper fluttered to my feet. I picked it up looking up and down the hall but there was nobody there. Shutting the door with my hip, I opened the paper. In the same small, perfect handwriting, James wrote, *You will be picked up at the time, on the day you noted.*

That night, as I lay in bed I felt the cool crisp paper under my pillow. I couldn't let go of the note and had to keep it close to know it was in fact real.

CHAPTER 17

I slept soundly the entire night. I couldn't even remember dreaming, simply closing my eyes and opening them again at seven o'clock in the morning. My hand was still hugging the paper under my pillow, and I smiled, knowing that even if my official date wasn't for another few days I would still see James that evening at work.

I had no time to waste. I needed to get moving. I had a nine thirty meeting with the finance office at the college. The bus ran at eight, twelve and three o'clock to the college so I needed to quickly get ready in order to make it to the bus stop for the morning ride. I turned the shower on and looked through the dresser for something to wear. The weatherman on the news had said this would be the beginning of a weeklong heatwave. It was easy to decide on a tank top and cut off shorts.

Ten minutes later I was throwing bread into the toaster. I twisted my hair into a bun, threw on makeup and quickly spread apple butter on my toast. As I checked my purse for my checkbook and paperwork that I needed for the meeting I ate the breakfast. Satisfied that I was all set, I stroked Sassy's back and grabbed a can of soda. I walked out the door with thirty minutes to make the bus.

I was the only one at the bus stop when Henry pulled up to the curb. I knew Henry as my Pap's friend from church.

"Annie! Great to see you," he said as I stepped through the door.

"You too Henry," I took a window seat toward the back of the bus. As Henry pulled away from the curb I got comfortable for the twenty five minute ride to the city.

There were three more stops until we made it to the convention center which was the final stop of the bus route. From there I would take a ten minute cab ride to the other side of the city and then walk across campus to the Finance office.

I was nervous. Even though informal, it still felt like an interview or at least what an interview would feel like if I ever had one. Working for Joey I had to promise to be on time and pinky swore to always be truthful. I was sure it was far from how a real interview would be like. I knew that this meeting was just another step in going back to school, and I would soon be able to check it off the to-do list; but it was difficult to know that within the next hour I would be writing off a huge amount of hard earned income.

As I sat in the leather chair outside of the finance office I told myself that the end result was worth the money.

The assistant called me into the office, and I formally met Carolyn Bradley, the Finance manager. She was dressed in a perfectly designed tan suit with a gold watch and diamond tennis bracelet that sparkled with every movement. She was soft spoken and gave a light handshake as she introduced herself. She was anything but informal. In my tank top and cutoffs, I immediately felt out of place. The room smelled like an old library, and the overly large desk seemed unusually small in the spacious office.

She pulled a file from the top of a stack and set it in front of her before rolling her chair up to the desk. She motioned to the leather seat on the opposite side.

"Ok, first, thank you for meeting with me Annie. We are very excited that you are joining us in the fall," she said as she opened the folder.

"I'm excited too…but nervous," I said, taking the seat she pointed to. It was cold to my bare legs.

She shuffled through the papers, "No need to worry, we're here to help any way we can. Now, let's talk about what you want to know most."

She pushed a paper across the table, "Here is what we have. You've selected Hotel and Restaurant management as your major, correct?"

I simply nodded my head and turned the page to look. It seemed reasonable, at least affordable for what I had in the bank. I also knew the applications for the grant and scholarships would be decided in another few weeks, plenty of time before classes started.

Carolyn pointed out that books were not included. I was still fine with the numbers.

She described the due dates and when to expect decisions on the paperwork submitted the week before. As I wrote the check she pushed other papers in my direction for signature. They included personal information for the file, emergency numbers and contact information, and plans for the schedule in the fall.

"Of course, once the scholarship and grant decision is made the total may change in your favor. We will then meet again at the end of the semester to review the amount due for winter," she said, repeatedly clicking the end of her pen.

I stopped in mid-signature. "Wait, this amount is for one semester, not through the end of the year?" I ask nervously.

If she noticed my anxiety it didn't show. "Correct, everything we deal with is in semesters. This keeps each department on the same schedule."

I rubbed my neck, and my mind began to race. I instantly got hot and the office, which once was massive, suddenly felt confined. I knew that what was left in savings would probably pay for the first year of school but would certainly not pay for books. I now depended on receiving a scholarship or the grant, and I never wanted to be in that position.

Quickly filling out the paperwork I knew I couldn't get out of the office fast enough. I needed to put a pen to the numbers. I accepted the papers that Carolyn offered me including one which showed the map of the campus. She had circled where the bookstore, academic office, and the library were. Apparently, sometime after the room collapsed on me she had mentioned where these places were and why I would need them.

Before I went to any of them I found the nearest bench and sat down digging in my purse for a pen and scrap of paper. I estimated that I would be about a thousand dollars short. I would hope for cheap used books. I knew I would probably be able to work a few hours at a local store or restaurant in addition to asking Joey for more hours, even though I knew he'd only be making them available for my benefit.

As disappointed as I was I knew I couldn't quit now. I had come too far, and I wasn't going to stop until I had a degree in my hand.

I walked around the campus looking at the points of interest that Carolyn had noted. Because it was summer the spacious campus was mostly deserted. Only a few students roamed around, most looking as lost as I was.

Coming to the top of a long stairwell, I stopped and stood completely still. I took a deep breath--just what I needed. It was a beautiful place and I was once again excited to get started. After seeing everything on the map that I needed to I picked up a hotdog from a street vendor and flagged down a taxi. I was ready to get home, and even more ready to see James.

When the bus arrived, Henry and I said our hellos again, and for this trip I took a seat at the front. As we were coming into town I could see a tall stack of long green pipes and heavy equipment in a field. The worker's trucks were parked along the highway. I strained my neck looking for the yellow hat among the men. I was disappointed when I couldn't locate James. It made me want to get home even more. Even though I know it wasn't true, I felt like the faster I could get there and go to work, the quicker I could see him.

When Henry pulled up to the curb I patted his shoulder, told him my goodbyes for the second time that day and ran down the stairs of the bus before he could even get the door open. I hurriedly made my way up the street and to my apartment.

I grabbed the mail, and sorted through flyers, magazines and bills as I watched cheesy talk shows. It was a bad habit I did before work, and I especially welcomed the distraction today. As Dr. Lonnie, a teen psychiatrist talked about depression in schools today I opened a letter from my sister. It was a quick note telling me they would be stateside soon and she would give me her new contact information then. She gave me a hint of where they were going by sending me a magazine clipping of orange juice.

Florida. Good for her.

I missed her and even if she would be as far south from Pennsylvania as she could get it was comforting to know that she was still going to be in the same country and more importantly in a same time zone.

CHAPTER 18

I found myself standing in the shower for the second time that day. As I stood under the heavy spray, I let the warm water massage my scalp. It felt so good that I didn't move until the water turned cold. I didn't even need the shower. I knew I wasn't only taking a marathon shower to get extra clean or to relieve stress, but I was also using it as a way to kill time. I've been doing that a lot lately.

Who in her right mind hurries to work?

Once again, I took extra steps in getting ready. I was making that a bad habit as well.

I dug through my drawer for the perfect necklace that matched the bracelet and earrings my grandma had given me years before, but I never found the occasion to need them. I put the perfect lip gloss on, and even used hot rollers to give my hair lift and fullness before pulling it up in an even more perfect French twist. I clipped it in place and sprayed the fly-a-ways down with hairspray. Then, upon inspection in the mirror, decided against the earrings and bracelet because it was too much for a smoky small-town bar.

A week from Tuesday was the 4th of July. This coming Sunday was the town's Independence Day celebration, and I was very excited. I was not like most people. If asked what their favorite holiday was most would say Christmas, or Easter, or even Halloween or Thanksgiving. You probably wouldn't be told Independence Day but it has always been my favorite holiday. I loved the fireworks, spending time with family and friends at a picnic, and especially the true meaning of the day.

Since starting work at Joey's, I dedicated the week before the 4th celebration as my personal way of observing the holiday. It gave me a reason to wear red, white, and blue each day. I loved my cutoff shorts that I wore that day so I recycled them with a different tank top. In holding true to my tradition, I chose a form fitting red ribbed tank top. The temperature was still in the ninety's, and it was to remain unseasonably hot all night long.

The window unit reminded me of just how hot it was. As I walked by, an arctic breeze brought goose bumps to my arms. I fed Sassy telling her to have a good night and to keep an eye on the place. Then as I made final adjustments to my outfit and sprayed the familiar pink bottle of perfume across my front I knew I couldn't do anything else to delay getting to work. I grabbed my purse and key, locked the door and just as I was about to close the door stopped and walked back inside. I quickly headed to the bedroom to find what I was looking for.

From the bedside table I grabbed the note that James left last night on my door and placed it in my left hip pocket. I wanted to keep it close. I left the apartment forty-five minutes before I needed to be at the bar. I really was pathetic.

CHAPTER 19

I unlocked the door of the bar and flipped on the light switches behind the window curtain. As the lights turned on from one end to the other, the place came to life. The air conditioner was running, and there was a slight chill in the air. It was cold now, but I'd welcome it later as the bar became more crowded.

I did an inspection of cleanliness in the restrooms, alcohol that was on hand, and ensured that the glasses were washed. Then, I started to cut lemons and limes and fill the snack bowls.

Just as I was filling the last one Joey walked in using his shirt collar to wipe his face. "It's a scorcher out there!"

"I see that," I said chuckling. "Thank goodness for air conditioning."

Sweat beaded back on his forehead. "I can't believe it's five o'clock and still ninety degrees."

I grabbed a handful of mixed nuts and chewed as I put the final touches on the prep work. Joey walked around the bar and discreetly asked, "So, where are you going on Thursday?" You could see him try to contain the laughter but unfortunately wasn't able to keep his secret of knowing about the date.

I coughed, choking on the nut mixture.

"He asked me where he should take you…. That's a real gentle-man you have there, Anna Banana." He laughed the whole way to the office.

I wished I could have melted into the floor at that moment. I was so shocked that even if I wanted to become defensive I was frozen in place with my mouth hanging open. I had to force it closed to keep the peanuts from falling out.

He knew. I was embarrassed, and it wasn't that I even cared that he knew; it was that I wasn't the one to tell him. That meant he and James were talking about me. My mind raced thinking about everything they could have talked about.

In a daze I cleaned up the empty containers from the nuts and the knife, and cutting board from the lemons and limes.

As if Joey knew the questions that flooded my mind he peaked around the corner. "Oh, and don't worry, we didn't talk about you. That was the only thing he asked."

I forced a laugh, covering up my anxiety, and just then Mickey walked in. "Well, your number one customer's just arrived… and first again I might add," he bellowed, looking around at the empty room.

"Hey Mickey," I called out.

I had his usual waiting for him before he slid into his seat. He took a long refreshing drink and commented on the heatwave. "Do you know it's the hottest it's been in over fifty years?" He asked.

I knew this subject was fodder for his stories. I just nodded and prepared myself for a long conversation.

He talked about the local farmers that would lose crops if it continued and the people that were rushed to the hospital from heat stroke. Within thirty minutes of his one-sided discussion a few more people had walked in.

By six o'clock all but two stools were full, and the customers kept me busy. Mickey had moved on to telling his story to others who mistakenly chose to sit near him.

Each time the door opened my heart stopped, and I turned around hoping to see James. By nine o'clock he hadn't arrived yet, and I was starting to worry he wasn't going to show tonight. I knew my mind wasn't with my work, and it wasn't like me to be distracted like that. Joey helped me at the bar and watched my reaction to each time the bell rang over the door.

"Hey, do you want to come over for lunch tomorrow? Kim has wanted me to ask you, and I keep forgetting," he said, pulling me back to reality.

I agreed but knew he had an ulterior motive. It was like the time he invited me to dinner only to discuss my new apartment situation, or the time his wife took me to lunch to ask about my plans for college. I liked spending time with them. I just wished they didn't feel the need to use invitations as a way to discuss important issues with me. Just like pseudo-adopted parents are supposed to do, I guess.

Vince, who was sitting at the right side of the bar also noticed my anxious glances toward the door. He called me over and whispered across the bar, "He's on his way. The site manager needed him to run into the city for some parts."

"Thank you," I smiled and whispered back.

Forty minutes later James walked in showered and without a baseball cap. He had also gotten a haircut, and I almost didn't notice him. He looked so sexy that I once again found myself with my mouth hanging open as I stood behind the bar tonight.

CHAPTER 20

That night I had a dream that took me back to my childhood. I was around six years old, and Laura and I had built a fort in the woods at our Aunt Ellen's house. We would visit her almost every weekend, and while my mom visited with her in the house we would sneak into the woods and hide. The fort was made of pine branches and scraps of old lumber. It was our home away from home and our place to just be kids. As messy as it was it was beautiful to us.

We would use piles of leaves for beds, logs as stools, and a rock was our imaginary television. We would tape pictures we drew to the front and "change channels" by changing pictures. We trampled the briars down to make a driveway and parked our bikes outside our front door – which was simply an old piece of fabric draped like a curtain.

The dream that night centered around an activity that we spent much of our time doing in the fort. Ellen had a flair for baking extravagant desserts, and we would pretend to be her in the kitchen making pies and cakes out of mud, sticks, and leaves. We would leave them on the picnic tables around the neighborhood and spy on the neighbors pretending to eat them. It was like I was there, fifteen years before. It felt so real again. I could smell the dirt and feel the breeze. We were making each dessert with precision and love, just as we watched Aunt Ellen do so many times.

As we delivered the last pie, walking toward an opening at the edge of the woods the scenery became new, different. This time instead of a backyard of another neighbor I looked up and saw a little boy standing in the middle of an open field. He was waving at us.

The glare of the sun suddenly became blinding, and even though

I still knew he was there I could barely see him. I shielded my eyes and walked in his direction. As I got closer he moved further away. I could hear him say my name, and I started to run in his direction. Just as I made it to him I heard someone call out for him to come home. He turned and ran away. I watched his red curls bounce in the other direction, and I tried to catch him but he disappeared.

I quickly opened my eyes and realized I was out of breath from running in my dream. I reached over and turned the alarm clock in my direction. It was a quarter till five. I sat up and drank from the glass of water I kept by my bed. What did the dream mean? Was the red-headed boy James?

It took twenty minutes for me to fall back asleep, and at eight o'clock I sat straight up in bed and felt the strong need to visit Gram and Pap. I needed my family.

After quickly getting dressed I called over to their house to make sure they would be home. Gram answered on the fourth ring.

"Hey Gram, what are you guys doing today," I asked.

"Nothing that I can think of, sweetheart. What's going on?"

"I thought I'd come see you," I said while playing with a marker that lay on the counter.

Gram didn't say anything for a few seconds. "Well that's a great surprise, Annie. It's not even Thursday."

"I know. I just needed to see you guys. How are you doing? How's Pap?"

"Well, I'm good, but your Pap hasn't felt very well lately. Maybe seeing you will cheer him up," she said.

I told her I'd be there in a little while, and we said our goodbyes. I called to cancel lunch with Joey telling him about my need to visit my grandparents. He understood, and within ten minutes I was on my bike and on the way to their house.

When I rode up to their driveway Gram was walking a letter to the mailbox, and Pap was rocking on the front porch. He looked pale and only quietly waved. Gram said she would be taking him to the doctor in the morning if he didn't get better, and I saw that sweat was beading on his forehead. It was only getting hotter as the morning grew on so I suggested we move inside.

I helped him up, and he slowly walked into the kitchen and he sat down. While I helped Gram with the dishes he read the newspaper. She asked me about James, and I filled her in on everything including the upcoming date for Thursday. She again gave her warnings of how men can be.

We laughed together, and I even heard Pap chuckling over the paper. I stayed for lunch, and just as we were about to say our good-byes I heard a glass fall to the floor, and looking in the direction of the sound I saw Pap hold his chest and stumble against the wall.

"Quick, call 911." Gram said rushing toward his side.

I ran to the phone and quickly dialed as I helped support him to sit down. He gasped to catch his breath.

Paramedics arrived just five minutes later. It seemed like five hours. The next ten minutes were a blur, and I found myself with my arm around Gram as she covered her mouth with both hands watching the ambulance with her husband race down the road toward the city.

CHAPTER 21

I grabbed the keys and helped my Gram into their car. It took a few tries to get it started. You could tell it had been a while since it had been driven.

We were only a few minutes behind the ambulance, but by the time we pulled up to the Emergency door he had already been unloaded from the ambulance and was taken inside.

Gram quietly sobbed as I helped her inside and sat her down in the closest chair. I rushed to the front desk to talk with the attendant. They could only tell me to wait until they called us back in.

As we waited I called Joey to let him know where I was and what was going on. He said he'd be there in a few minutes. Then I used my calling card to call Laura. I had to leave a message, and as I listened to the beep I changed my mind and simply said I'd call back later. I didn't want to worry her if I wasn't even sure what was happening myself.

As Gram and I sat in silence watching a muted talk show I felt a tap on my shoulder. I jumped as I turned around.

"Are you John Green's granddaughter?" the nurse asked.

Standing I quickly replied, "Yes, and this is my grandma, Ruth."

She pulled up a chair and opened a clipboard, "He is stable. I think we caught the heart attack early enough, but we need to get him into surgery. At least three of his arteries… blocked… bypass… permission… immediately."

It all was getting foggy.

She handed me the clipboard and instructed me on everything that needed to be completed. The last thing I heard was that they were wheeling him upstairs, and that once we filled out the registration paperwork we could wait in the ICU waiting room until he was out of surgery.

As I filled out page after page and Gram signed where I instructed Joey rushed in to meet us. He hugged both of us, and I filled him in on what was happening. Because he would need to get to the bar he could only spare a few hours. He sat in virtual silence with us until four o'clock, and as he hugged me he whispered that I didn't need to come in until at least Friday. He'd call me for an update that evening.

When he left, Gram and I tried to make conversation, but it was hard to concentrate without knowing what was going on. In a daze I stared at the television until the door opened, and the doctor approached with a friendly smile.

He said everything went perfectly, and Pap's heart was as good as new. I hugged Gram, and the relief was so great she started to cry on my shoulder.

"I just don't know what I would have done if I lost him," she whispered.

"Me too," I said.

We looked in on him when allowed. He was groggy but alert enough to give a frail thumbs-up when we walked in the room. It made us laugh and Gram gripped his hand gently pulling it to her chest. He moaned as if in pain, but then smiled to let her know he was ok.

I patted his arm and kissed his forehead thanking him for not leaving us. Then I left Gram and Pap alone to just be together. They needed that time.

I called Laura back, and this time I got her. She said she tried to call but there was no answer. I told her I was still at the hospital and then explained what brought us there. We talked for another thirty minutes, and as I hung up and picked up the remote to change channels there was a knock at the door.

"It's after seven and I knew you probably didn't eat dinner so I brought it to you." To my left, James spoke softly as he handed a large paper bag through the doorframe.

He had brought a variety of salads and sandwiches from a nearby deli.

"I'm not sure what you like, so I brought some of everything," he said as I unpacked the contents laying them on the coffee table.

"How did you know where I was?" I asked.

"Word made it around the place fast. All the guys send their best too." He sat on the edge of the chair opposite me.

I chose a Greek salad and bottle of water. "Thank you, James. You didn't have to do this, but I appreciate your thoughtfulness."

"No problem, really."

I told him what was going on with Pap, and then he stood and said he had to leave.

"Oh… you can't stay for a while?" I asked.

He shook his head, "Nah, I need to get up early tomorrow. I have to be onsite at four thirty in the morning. And you need to spend time with your family."

I reached forward and hugged him, thanking him again for the food. He relaxed against me and encircled my body into his chest. It was a perfect twenty seconds.

"I will see you soon Annie. I'm praying for your grandpa," he said, quickly pulling away and leaving the waiting room.

Visiting hours ended at eight o'clock. Gram sat with me in the waiting room eating an egg salad sandwich that James brought and she raved about how nice it was of him to do such a thing. With the large selection he brought there would be enough for at least the next day, if not two.

By nine thirty we were back at her house, and I realized that I was exhausted. I couldn't imagine how Gram felt. The emotions and excitement of the day had drained us.

I put the leftovers in the refrigerator and then hugged Gram goodnight. I told her I'd be on the couch if she needed anything and then closed my eyes, falling asleep before my head hit the pillow.

CHAPTER 22

Two distinct things woke me up, peaking my senses. First, was the smell of bacon frying, and the second was the sound of loud banging on the back door.

"Yes, yes… no, I haven't heard anything else… come in," I heard Gram say to someone standing on the porch.

Once the unknown person entered and they continued their conversation I immediately recognized the airy voice of Elizabeth, Pap's youngest sister. Gram must have called the family first thing that morning.

I straightened my clothes, finger combed my hair, and walked into the kitchen to greet both women.

"Annie! Good gracious! Look at you. You're so beautiful even after sleeping in your clothes," Elizabeth said, rushing to give me a hug.

"Thanks, Liz…I think," I said, squeezing her back.

Elizabeth was sixty-five but looked and acted like a woman in her mid-forties. She was a retired fashion designer but still taught night classes on the subject at the local college. She power-walked every day and drove a convertible. I hoped to one day be half as vibrant as she was.

We ate breakfast--well attempted to eat breakfast--although mainly we pushed the food around on the plates and sipped coffee while watching the clock. Visiting hours didn't start until ten o'clock, and we were just buying time.

While Gram retold the story of what happened, I borrowed her car and drove home for a shower and to change clothes. Because I was gone since yesterday morning, I also had to feed a now starving Sassy.

I felt a million times better as I was retracing my drive back to

Gram's thirty minutes later. I also had a wave of good feeling pass over me, and I knew that Pap was going to be ok. I quietly prayed a little thank you and met Liz and Gram just was they were walking in to the hospital.

As soon as I saw Pap I knew I was right. He looked remarkable. He'd gotten all color back in his cheeks and was joking with the nurse when we all walked in.

"My girls!" he exclaimed, wincing slightly in pain.

He gently hugged each one of us, and the nurse explained that if today went as well as last night they would probably downgrade him to a regular room for the rest of his stay.

"Wonderful news!" Liz said, excusing herself for being so loud. "Sorry, but I knew John was always too tough to go down that easy."

We spent the day taking turns sitting with Pap during visiting hours and gossiping in the waiting room while awaiting our time with him. We would take turns running back to the house to eat and walking outside in the visitor's park when we needed fresh air.

By six o'clock I realized I should be at work. As I sat by the fountain watching a young couple across from me holding hands and talking I wondered if that is how Gram and Pap were. Last night, when she sat beside him I could see the same passion that had probably brought them together many years before.

I became jealous of what they, as well as, another couple across the water fountain obviously had. Watching them sit close and stare into each other's eyes I knew that is exactly what I wanted in a relationship.

"Hey sweetness," Elizabeth said, walking up beside me. "Whatcha thinking about?"

"That." I motioned across to the other couple. "They are so happy. I hope one day I have that."

She chuckled. "Girl, you are so young, so smart, and not to mention so pretty, you have nothin' to worry about in that department."

We talked about how she and Uncle Ron met. They were another couple that seemed so happy in a world where lasting marriages were becoming few and far between. When she asked if there was anyone special in my life I started to say no, but she knew I was lying, as she always could tell, so I told the story of James and how even without having a date and only knowing him for a little over a week I felt closer to him than any other guy.

As Wednesday night grew closer I said my goodbyes to the family. I needed to make it back to Gram and Pap's before dark so I could ride my bike home. Elizabeth promised to take care of Gram and explained that she packed for a week but would stay longer if needed. I said to expect a call in the morning. As I walked out the door Liz pulled me aside and whispered that I had to also promise her something, that I would just forget about everything and have a good time with James on the date tomorrow night. I smiled and agreed knowing I needed to, but also hoping I could.

CHAPTER 23

I didn't sleep. Period. I had a million thoughts running in my head and a million more chasing them. Just as I started to ease the nerves from thinking about the date, Pap's drawn up face from the agonizing pain of the heart attack took the place in my head.

Eventually I took a walk in the dark from my bedroom to the couch and clicked on the television. Nothing but infomercials and old reruns were available to choose from. I landed on a black and white romance movie and settled in for the remainder of the night.

As dawn approached I made my coffee and sat in my usual chair on the porch hoping the workers would stop at the bakery next door, but it was quiet, too quiet, and I needed to find out how Pap was doing.

I called the hospital. They told me his night was uneventful which was good, but they couldn't say much more until the doctor made his rounds. In the seven o'clock hour I couldn't wait any longer. I got on the bike and pedaled hard and fast making it to Gram's house within ten minutes. She and Liz were sitting at the table when I knocked on the door.

"Annie? Honey? What are you doing here? I thought I said to take the day for just you," Liz said, opening the door.

"I just needed to be here." I was out of breath.

"Come in, child," Gram said, getting up from the table.

As I sat down I told them about my night. "I have had no sleep... just thinking about everything kept me up...and you're my only family around here. It's lonely being there wondering what's happening. That's why I felt like I needed to come here."

Gram put her cold hands on mine. "You know what? Pap will

be fine. He is tough, determined, and not ready to leave me yet. He does want you to be happy as well, and he knows you aren't ignoring him by having a life of your own."

"I know. I'm just torn. I feel like I need to be there for him," I said, rubbing her hands.

She quickly answered, "And you are. You just don't need to hole yourself up in the hospital to prove it."

Her comment made me laugh, and she asked what was funny. I was remembering back to when I was twelve, and mom was in the hospital for that final stay.

"Do you remember the last time I was at the hospital? Mom was there, and it was the last weeks she was with us."

Gram simply nodded.

"Mom was so mad that she had to be there. She wanted to go home, but the doctors were determined that she was to stay. So we moved her house to her.

Each day we brought something new, from the pictures on the walls to the books, her slippers, alarm clock, and even that crazy lawn chair and fake grass. She wanted to be at home in the backyard more than anything. The day we brought that chair in her smile lit the room. She even cried she was so happy." I stopped, looking down at our hands touching.

Gram saw I was sad but simply continued the story for me. "And coupons. We had to bring her the Sunday paper each week just for her to clip those darn coupons. We had shoeboxes of those things. I don't think we ever even had the time to use a single one of them. We were at that hospital day and night."

Gram stopped talking, and I sighed. Liz caressed my hair. "That's why we're not going to move back into a hospital ever again. If John wants to see his stuff from his house again he'll have to come home. Now get back on that bike and ride back home. Take a bubble bath, give yourself a manicure, and shave those legs for your hot date." She winked for added affect.

All three of us laughed. Gram promised to give me a full report when they got there, and I promised the same the next morning from my night before.

I felt much better on my ride home and smiled the entire way. I even caught myself whistling as I opened the door and greeted Sassy. I shook my head after figuring what I was whistling... "The Sun'll come out Tomorrow."

CHAPTER 24

I ran my fingers along the yellow stitching on the sun dress. The thread felt course compared to the soft cotton of the white material it decorated. I was nervous and anxious, and both were making me sick in my stomach as I stood in front of the mirror staring at my reflection. It was five thirty, and I was completely dressed and ready with nothing to do but count the minutes until James arrived.

I sat on the couch all afternoon after arriving back to the apartment from visiting Gram and Aunt Liz. Hours of talk shows, game shows, and commercials occupied my time, but after catching myself staring blankly at a divorce judge, I finally realized I couldn't watch anything else. I spent forty minutes in the shower until the water ran cold and then just as long matching the right pair of shoes to my new dress.

I dried and curled my hair and dug through an old drawer of makeup pulling out the lip liner and brow comb, neither of which had seen the daylight since prom night my senior year. I fluffed, sprayed, combed, brushed, fixed, and re-fixed until every last hair was exactly how I wanted. I checked the mirror, double checked, triple checked, and finally made myself walk away from the bathroom.

Now, with an hour and a half left I sat at the table and looked from side to side not wanting to move even my head an inch for fear I might mess up something. Out the window I could see the sun was shining and the wind was nonexistent. Good. I wouldn't need to worry about a breeze messing up my hair.

Sassy purred beside me, and the clock on the counter ticked softly. I lightly tapped my fingers to the beat, and it didn't take but a few minutes to grow boring so I stood back up knowing this was going to be the longest ninety minutes of my life.

To pass the time I called the hospital to check on Pap. He was now in a downgraded room and in great spirits. Gram filled him in on the date, and he gave me a list of questions to ask him and hints on what to look for. Then, as he was hanging up he wished me the best of luck and asked that I come see him in the morning.

"Of course, Pap. I'll be there as soon as they let me in the door," I said, sending my love as I hung up.

That only took seven minutes.

So I called Kate. She wasn't home, so I left a message telling her about Pap and thanking her once again for helping me find the dress.

So, another thirty-eight seconds went by.

Laura! It would be early in the morning in South Korea but I would wake her up if needed.

She answered on the fourth ring.

"It's not Pap, is it?" She asked, not even saying a hello.

"No, he's fine. In fact, he's moved out of the ICU he's doing so well," I answered.

"Good. I didn't mean to think the worst." She sighed with obvious relief.

"I just wanted to talk to you. I haven't in a while, and I wanted to catch you before you headed out for the day."

She explained that they were busy getting ready for the move. His papers had them leaving in two weeks, so there was a lot of packing they needed to do.

"So, what are you up to?" She asked, and I could hear her whisper to Matt in the background saying a goodbye as he left for work.

I let them finish their quiet conversation before starting my story of James. She knew very little about the workers and nothing about how he asked me out and that we would be going on a date today.

"Awwww, my baby sister is growing up so fast," she joked.

"Shut up!" I said, as any sister would.

"No, really, I am happy for you, Annie. You deserve to be happy, especially having as much on your plate as you do. Go have fun tonight. Just don't find too much fun. Fun leads to trouble, you know."

I laughed. "I love you, Laura. I hope to see you soon,"

"I love you, and I hope to see you soon, too," she said.

We said our good-byes and I looked at the clock. Getting there - only twenty minutes left.

Ten minutes later though there was a quiet knock on the door. He was early. I took a deep breath then quickly turned the handle. He took one look at me in the dress, and the hello he was going to say stopped at his lips and his jaw fell.

"You don't look too bad yourself," I said.

I saw that he chose the black polo from his shopping trip. It was perfect. He saw me looking at his outfit.

Pointing at his shirt, I said, "And I'm glad you didn't pick the red one."

My comment confused him. He stood there with a puzzled look on his face. As I turned to close the door behind me he caught sight of the plunging neckline on the back of my dress. His eyes opened wide competing with his now gaping mouth. He remained speechless.

CHAPTER 25

As we made it to the bottom of the stairs and headed out the front door I expected to find Joey's borrowed truck or the town's sole taxi cab with sixty-five-year-old Leonard behind the wheel. Instead a black limousine with dark tinted windows and a driver extending his hand toward the open back door greeted us.

As I walked toward him he gently nodded his head with his fingers holding the tip of his hat. His voice was soft when he spoke. "Evening ma'am."

James placed his hand on the small of my back and helped me into the limo. It immediately sent a chill racing along my spine.

Soft music was playing, and there was an open bottle of champagne and two glasses in the holder. I made room for James as the driver got behind the wheel and raised the divider window. We were alone in the dimly lit backseat.

"I can't believe you did all this." I took the glass he offered.

As he poured himself a glass he gave a half grin. "It's not too often I have a date. From what I understand the same is true for you, so I thought we deserved a nice evening."

"Well, whatever you have planned next can't be better than this."

He simply extended his half grin before taking a big gulp of champagne.

I watched the town's lights disappear, and I knew we were on our way into the city. Along the ride he asked questions that you could tell were lingering in his mind to ask: What were my favorite colors, music, hobbies, and movies. With each question I asked the same of him banking everything in my memory for further use.

He told a story of dancing with his mom at a friend's wedding when he was in grade school and how Louis Armstrong's What a Wonderful World became his favorite song because of that moment.

My heart felt like it was going to explode right there. What a touching vision. Knowing that secret was so tender and special to him, and he was sharing it with me which was remarkable. I believe that was the exact moment I realized there were more than innocent feelings that I had for him. This also made the evening even more phenomenal to me.

I began to loosen my anxiety strings that helped me from being who I truly was, and before I knew it the 30 minutes we were in the limo flew by. When I looked out the window we were parking along the curb of an alley-facing restaurant. The doorman opened the limo door and offered the plain black entryway to us. Inside James leaned in and whispered to the hostess and I assumed he gave his name.

As she directed us to follow her I looked around at the other patrons and admired the quaint furnishings and subtle wall hangings. Most customers were seated at the long bar or the small pub tables around the room. The room was relatively small and within 25 steps we had made it to the far wall.

Continuing to follow the hostess, she took us through another doorway leading outside, and I realized we were now entering the true essence of the restaurant. A narrow walkway wound around the bank toward the river below. Along the route the walk branched off giving way to secluded dining areas. Couples were given privacy to dine and each table faced a stage set along the water's edge. The foliage and flowered bushes were strategically placed so each couple felt like they were the only ones there viewing the entertainment and were dining alone. It was unbelievable. I had never seen anything so beautiful. A jazz band was playing on the stage, and when we arrived at our table toward the left of the stage I saw a perfectly set table with a bottle of wine chilling to the side.

"Welcome to the Gardens Restaurant," the hostess said. Her name tag read Becky in perfect calligraphy.

"Your menus are at your place setting. When ready press the button in the middle and someone will be here to take your order." She motioned where everything was.

"Enjoy the entertainment. And if you need anything don't hesitate to ask." And within seconds she disappeared.

I took it all in. Beside the table set a cushioned glider. Sitting in the middle on the flowered seat was a small bowl of chocolate covered strawberries. I understood then where they thought dessert would be served.

James cleared his throat, and when I turned I saw him holding out my chair.

"I'm so sorry. I am just amazed with this place. How did you ever find it?" I asked, taking the chair that was offered.

"Joey," he answered. "He brought his wife here to ask her to marry him."

If I was drinking at that moment I would have sprayed the table. It was my turn. I was now speechless.

CHAPTER 26

I spent the first twenty minutes of the date sitting in silence. I was scared, anxious, and anything but hungry. I had stared blankly at the menu, and I vaguely remember opening my mouth and allowing words to fall out. I don't really remember, but I think I ordered a chicken and pasta dish. It was the first thing I saw on the menu when the waiter arrived at our table. I would know for certain when they delivered it.

James was just as quiet. He knew what he had said about Joey's proposal made me nervous. If nothing else the size that my eyes had grown was a dead giveaway. He had tried to laugh it off, but he appeared to become more uncomfortable.

When a new band took the stage the music selection changed to an upbeat salsa swing. It was exactly what we needed to turn the mood around.

"So, how is work at the site going?" I encouraged the conversation to move along while taking a long sip from my wine glass.

He drank as well and after licking the wine from his lips answered, "Good. The site manager said we were progressing along well. With two crews it hasn't been taking long to do the work."

I knew that meant that the quicker they got done, the quicker he would leave, but I didn't let it dampen my mood. I took another long drink and collected my thoughts. "Do they have any plans for the crew after you finish here? I mean what's next for you?"

"I really don't know. The next meeting isn't until Monday morning. I'm hoping to know more then." He paused for a few seconds before continuing, "I know it doesn't matter where they send me. It'll be too far away."

I blushed and looked at the glass I rolled in my hands. I felt the exact same way.

The waiter silently interrupted with salads and a basket of bread. He slipped out just as quickly as he entered, and I realized that this was indeed the perfect date place, and in the twenty-one years of my life I never even knew it existed.

As if he read my mind James commented, "This is a great place, isn't it?"

I nodded while separating the hard crust from the bread in front of me.

James continued to talk as I took a bite. "Joey told me you have all but started attending school now that you know what your first class will be when fall comes."

Swallowing, I answered, "Yes, now I'm just waiting on the financial aid, and I'm trying to figure the money out and ..."

I stopped in mid-sentence. "But you don't want to know all those details."

"Yes, I do. That's why I asked."

I cleared my throat. "Well let's just say that if I don't get the financial aid needed I don't know how I'll get to go. I'm almost ten thousand dollars short of obtaining my goal."

Saying the amount out loud was difficult to hear. I was pretending the conversation with the admissions woman hadn't happened and just crossed my fingers that everything would come through for me. I took another drink finishing my glass. James had the bottle waiting for me.

"You don't need to worry, it will all work out," he said, setting the bottle down and resting his hand on mine. He quickly pulled it away and picked up his piece of bread.

I watched him nervously pick at the slice of bread in front of him and start to de-crust it. Little crumbs were left on the plate which now looked like mine.

Just like mine. As childish as I probably sounded I told myself that it just had to be fate.

CHAPTER 27

The dinner we ordered was beautifully presented and tasted perfect. I didn't know if it was the company I was with or the setting, but the flavors were extraordinary. And I was right. I had ordered the blackened chicken pasta.

Dessert involved a cart of fresh fruit and chocolate fondue in addition to the chocolate covered strawberries. As you are finishing up your meal the staff is quietly setting up the other side of your dining area in preparation for the rest of the evening.

Knowing that we were using the area for quite a while meant that this date probably cost James a pretty penny. I was always concerned with the cost of things and the money being spent.

It was a terrible habit I had. I know I needed to let go and just have a good time and this included everything in my life, but I was always too busy checking prices and hunting a bargain to really enjoy myself. This is probably why as I now sat and stared at James I was mostly looking through his eyes and into space wondering about my large tuition bill that sat in my college account.

"You look distracted. Is everything okay?" James asked.

Coming back into the moment I took a deep breath and noted the salsa music had been toned down to a soft slow number. "Yeah, I'm just taking this all in."

"Well how about another dance?"

The last time I was swaying around the floor in his arms had been in the bar when he played Annie's Song from the jukebox. I smiled remembering the butterflies I felt at that time.

I took his hand, and he quickly pulled me close to him. I felt his racing heart through my thin dress, and I wondered if he felt mine too. It was like two beating drums trying to stay in tune with one another. I couldn't pinpoint if it was all the wine or being close to him again, but I was dizzy as he spun me around, and the feelings of butterflies grew ten-fold in my stomach.

I stopped the two of us mid turn and looked up into his eyes. I no longer could hear the music only our hearts beating in unison. As if reading my mind, he leaned down and kissed my lips pulling me even closer into him.

As quickly as he started the kiss I ended it. It wasn't that I wanted to, but my knees began to buckle so fast I had to catch myself from collapsing in front of him.

"Whoa now... Let's sit down." He caught me and directed us to the glider.

I followed, not having much of a choice. He pulled the tray of dessert toward us.

"I think what you need is some sugar." He handed me a forked skewer holding a ripe strawberry on the end.

With the sweet kiss still fresh in my mind I didn't hesitate to answer. "I don't know about that... sugar's what just took me to my knees."

CHAPTER 28

B esides the company, the best part of the night so far had to be the dessert. The chocolate was so rich and creamy that I couldn't stop dipping the fruit and eating. James had stopped long before and was now relaxed back on the glider with his right arm resting on the back and sipping a flute of champagne with the other.

Instead of watching the band on the stage out front he stared at me as I chewed each bite. Each time I made a sighing sound or yum of approval he would giggle. Finishing off the last piece of pineapple I chased the bite with a long drink from my glass. I was beyond full, and leaning back I snuggled close to James' ribcage. He covered my right side with his arm and pulled me closer.

"Are you cold?" he asked.

"No, full, but not cold, not yet anyway," I said.

I glanced at the night sky and could just make out the stars disguised by the city lights. It wasn't like at home. I could sit on my deck and count to infinity with the shining lights above my head. The light pollution from the industry and commercial buildings prevented the true beauty of the stars from being revealed.

It was sad to know that even though we all lived on the same earth some people didn't have the same sky that we did out in the country.

"It is a nice night," James commented, noticing me looking above. "Would you like to walk down by the water after this last band finishes?"

"That would be great. I haven't done that since…since…my mom was still alive. She loved the water, said it was the reason she was drawn to the lakefront property we had in Virginia." I smiled, thinking about the story she once told me.

"Tell me all about her." He encouraged me to go on.

"Well, she was absolutely beautiful, inside and out. There is no other way to describe her. She was firm, don't get me wrong, but I know now that everything she said to me and my sister had a lesson behind it. Guess a person takes that for granted when they are young." I stopped, watching the bubbles rise in my glass and collecting my thoughts.

The same time the band announced their final song and thanked everyone for coming. They wished everyone luck and even more love, because you just didn't know where the world would take you. I closed my eyes and slowly nodded. It was fitting considering our conversation we were having.

As they played a final ballad I began again. "When I was eight or nine she took me and my sister to get our pictures made. She didn't know she was sick then, and I'm not sure if she was intuitive with what was to come or not, but she just had to have pictures made. We didn't have any fancy outfits on, and from what I remember probably didn't even have our hair combed, but as a spur of the moment decision drove us to the studio and told the photographer that if she had to wait an hour she was getting our pictures made that day. As luck had it, and unfortunately my mom didn't have much of that in her life, the people that were to be there at that time didn't show up so she was able to fit us in.

"Well the photographer took about twenty poses of us, and with each one my mom's smile grew bigger. For the last one the lady asked her if she wanted to join us. She kept saying no, but my sister and I made her. I'm so glad she did. It was the last picture we had taken together." I pulled out the worn picture from my wallet and showed James. "And I carry it with me everywhere I go."

He turned toward me and wrapped his other arm around me, hugging me tightly. He didn't have to say anything, and I didn't expect him to. Actually, his hug was exactly what I needed.

As the band played the final note he released me. "Let's go for that walk now," he said.

CHAPTER 29

The theater setting of the tables was separated with a winding walkway ending at the water's edge on either side of the stage. As we made our way down the path James held my hand and helped me over the stepped areas. His rough hands had a surprisingly gentle feel to them. His grip was light, and he unintentionally rubbed his thumb along the back of my hand. It sent a tingle along my spine.

As we exited the gate close to the water I was shocked at the view. It was breathtaking. The lights of the city reflected off the river's surface, and the sound of light waves crashed along the rock-lined shore. Perfect. I pulled my hand from his and rubbed my arms reacting to the temperature difference by the water.

Instantly James removed his jacket and quickly placed it over my shoulders. He squeezed my arms.

"Is that better?" he asked.

"Yes, thank you so much," I said, turning to look at him.

The lighted waves cast shadows on his face and his eyes glimmered. Immediately I was warmed up to the point of sweating.

"So, tell me more about your childhood." He released the tension between us.

As we walked by the river he again took my hand, and I chose to tell him the hardest story of my past.

"When I found out my mom was moving us to Pennsylvania I was devastated. I remember not talking to her for weeks because she took me from my friends, my school, my house. About a week after we moved into my Gram's house I even ran away," I said.

He slowed down and looked at me. "What? You ran away? Where did you go?"

"Not far." I laughed. "I packed everything I needed, or let me rephrase that, everything a twelve-year-old needed like a toothbrush, a change of clothes, my diary, and a few music tapes. I did remember to take the map from my mom's car. As I made it to the first crossroads, about five blocks away I realized the map I had grabbed was the one from Virginia."

James chuckled and I continued. "So, I guessed and turned right, and within fifteen minutes realized I made it to the road behind Gram's house. I was mad, upset, but also in a way convinced that someone," and I looked up and pointed to the sky, "was making me stay here. So, I sat on the back steps for the next hour and cried knowing I'd never see my Virginia life again. Sitting in that same spot I overheard my mom tell Gram that the doctor diagnosed her with cancer, and that she didn't have much time. They didn't know I was sitting there. And all I kept thinking about was that just a little while ago I was leaving this place behind." I paused and stared out over the water.

James squeezed my hand letting me know he was listening. "I will never forget the sickening feeling I had, how life stood still. Everything went silent, and even the leaves seemed to stop blowing on the trees. When everything started to move again I was in denial, and in a way I even thought it was a joke. I got up and went back into the house. My mom was in her room and my Gram was staring blankly into a pot of boiling water. I turned the television on and remember watching Tom and Jerry. I have no idea why I remember that.

It was not until later that day that they sat me and my sister down and told us what I already knew. Crazy, but it hurt as much as if I didn't know."

"My grandma was diagnosed with cancer when I was really young too, and although it wasn't my mom I was close to her too, and I can remember that same sick feeling," James offered. "I am so sorry about your loss though."

"No, I'm okay. It took a long time, but it made me strong, the person I am today. And I know she would be very proud of me and where I'm going with my life. She always wanted us to go to college.

I just wish she could be there when I start...and when I finish," I say.

"She will be, even if you don't see her you'll know she is there. I talk to my grandma all the time, and I believe, even if it's just to make me feel better, that she hears me," he said.

"I feel the same way."

I wondered if mom was watching over me and smiling as I stood there staring at James and falling in love.

CHAPTER 30

As if he read my mind James leaned down and kissed me gently on the lips. He pulled me close, wrapping his arms around my waist. As his kiss intensified his grip grew tighter. Eventually we molded together as if we were one person.

Minutes passed, and I held his waist not wanting to let go.

A boat's horn sounded as it approached the dock nearby interrupting our moment. I opened my eyes and pulled away at the same time ripping me from my sensual feeling. I knew I should stop, that just a little over a week and a half ago I didn't even know this man existed. So, these feelings...these desires...were not supposed to happen. Not yet anyway.

Now, back from fairytale land I sighed deeply and pointed to a coffee cart along the boardwalk.

"Let's get a cup of coffee."

"Perfect idea. It will go great with our next plan." He smiled.

I furrowed my eyebrows wondering what was in store.

We each ordered a small coffee with cream and continued down the shoreline. With his hand on my back he led me to where the boat was docking. The captain waved in our direction, and as I turned to look behind me to see who he was motioning to. I saw James wave back.

As we approached the edge of the dock James helped me on to the boat, and the captain cocked his worn and crooked hat, nodding. "Good evening, ma'am."

"Good evening," I answered.

The boat was a small cruiser with the words 'Skyline Fishing and Touring Company' on the side.

"Sorry, it's the only one I could find on such short notice," James said, as he climbed on board.

"So, we are fishing tonight?" I laughed.

James shook his head. "No, we'll actually be doing the touring part."

We took two seats in the back of the boat, and I sipped on my coffee.

A few minutes later another couple came on board and sat at the front. With the four of us seated, the captain spoke into the intercom, welcoming us aboard.

"We will spend the next ninety minutes together on this night cruise. I will tell you about this city, the river, and the history of the area. In the next few minutes we will pull away from the dock and begin the trip. Does anyone need anything or have any questions?" he asked.

When nobody said anything he slowly backed the boat up from the dock and we began to head down the river. As soon as we moved forward the captain began by introducing himself and beginning his speech. "My name is Charlie, and I am your captain. Just to let you know, you are sitting on the oldest tour boat on this river," he exclaimed.

As the captain talked, James and I stared at the city from the unique vantage point that most people would never get to experience. The place was alive with people, music poured from the shoreline, and the lights illuminated the sky. Living in a town so close to all of this I never got to really experience it. I didn't party at the bars, dance at the clubs, or even sightsee. I was working more than play-ing. I hoped not being able to participate in the fun like the others would all pay off in the end.

"I want to go there." James pointed at a teal blue lighted building rising high above the others on the block.

As if Charlie read his mind he described the exact building and noted that it was one of the largest museums in the North East. "They have everything from dinosaurs to futuristic space equipment," he said.

"Let's plan to do that then. Sounds like a great second date," I joked.

We laughed, and I cuddled closer into his shoulder. He held me against his side, and we listened quietly as Charlie told about the history of the large coal mine in town and how the freight is still shipped down river as it was for many decades before.

I watched the other couple in front of us. They weren't paying any attention to us or to Charlie. They kissed, laughed, and whispered into each other's ears, and I wondered if they were a new couple, or was that behavior years in the making?

We listened to Charlie quietly for the next few minutes. Shutting off the engine he instructed us to stop and take in the sounds of the city at night. I thought about Pap in his hospital room a few blocks away, and how Gram probably just left his side missing him the minute she walked away. And I thought of my sister yearning to bring her family back to America. And now, this other couple, who I never met and didn't know from the next two people; but I could see the power that love had over them. With James by my side I knew that I too wanted that special someone in my life. I was ready to share my life and that I didn't want to be alone anymore. I didn't think I could go back to that.

Charlie started talking, and James, while still looking out the window, told me a story of the first time he was on a boat.

"I was learning to fish," he said. "My best friend Mark's dad owned a little fishing boat, and we were probably seven or eight, and he took us out on it one summer day. I caught the trees, the rocks, the motor, but not one fish. I was so frustrated that I gave up about fifteen minutes into it. Then, just as we were riding back to the inlet where the dock was to load up and go home I tried one more time by the bank as we waited for Mark's dad to pull the boat out, and you know what? I caught a ten-inch bass. For some reason that memory just came back to me. I guess it just goes to show you that you don't have to go out into the big lake to find what you're looking for. It might be in the small cove all along."

I don't know if his story had an alternate meaning behind it but for some reason I felt like a ten-inch bass at that moment.

CHAPTER 31

The boat ride was surprisingly exciting, and Charlie was full of information. I had learned more about the city in those ninety minutes than the entire time I lived with my grandparents. I now knew the oldest living woman in the state lived here. She was one hundred and twelve. What was even more surprising was her husband just died last year, and he was the second oldest person at one hundred ten.

I learned about the sports teams, famous musicians from the area, and the record temperatures that scorched the pavement to a gooey mess and froze the river solid. By the time we had turned around and were heading back James and I, as well as the unknown couple in the front were fully engrossed and hung on every word Charlie said. He was a wonderful speaker, and even though he had probably recited the same speech each trip downstream, he had perfected a way to make it interesting and seem so unrehearsed.

James switched from holding my hand to wrapping his arm around me. By the time we pulled back into the dock he had embraced me in a tight hug and held me close to his chest shielding me from the cool river breeze.

He led me to the front and helped me to the dock. As we passed Charlie I thanked him for a wonderful trip. James shook his hand and in his palm gave Charlie a tip letting him know his appreciation for the tour.

As we walked up the path I saw the limo waiting at the top of the sidewalk. I was so impressed that James had planned, and executed, such a wonderful evening. I looked at him and smiled stopping in the middle of the walk. "And thank YOU for a great time tonight."

"Anytime, Annie," he said. "Anytime."

He held open the door of the limo, and within a few seconds we were on the way back home. Passing the theater where we just ate hours ago, I smiled again.

James handed me a glass of wine. I wasn't a big drinker and before that night had never had a glass. The red wine earlier was sweet and smooth. I expected this white kind to be the same. Instead, it was tart. It wasn't bad, just slightly sour, and I realized I was puckering my lips.

James laughed. "Sorry, it wasn't my first pick of wine either."

"No, no, it's very good." I lied, "just not as sweet as I usually drink."

I turned my face away from him and chugged down the wine in two gulps. Immediately I felt light headed, but as I was getting my eyes to straighten out James had refilled my glass.

I sighed slowly out of my nose knowing I made two mistakes by drinking so fast. First my glass was refilled before I could swallow and second, I was on a quick road to being drunk for only the second time in my life.

CHAPTER 32

When we got back to the apartment I stumbled out of the limo and then giggled uncontrollably at my blunder. I knew it was close to midnight if not past that, and I felt my eyelids growing heavier. I'm sure the alcohol didn't help, and I allowed James to help me to my door.

After fumbling with the key in the lock he held my hand and guided it into place turning it, and the distinct click echoed letting me know the deadbolt had been opened. I turned and focused on James' face. He was smiling and apologized again for the wine.

"I had a great time tonight James," I said.

"Me too." He looked at his watch and noting it was indeed after twelve said, "I'll see you tonight at work. Now get some sleep, ok?"

To simply answer him I leaned up, grabbed his neck and kissed him long and slowly. He wrapped me in his arms and kissed me back.

We stood there like that for a long time. In the distance we could hear footsteps on the stairs. We broke the kiss, and I looked up at him. "I'll see you later James." I turned and quickly entered my apartment. I leaned against the door as Sassy crisscrossed through my legs. I could hear James talking to the person that walked up the stairs. Then, within a few minutes it was quiet.

I washed my face and brushed my teeth. Quickly changing my clothes, I fed Sassy and stroked her back as she ate, purring between bites.

I told her about my evening. She was a good listener. "James is like a Prince Charming yet I don't really feel like a deserving princess. I know, I know, I should just enjoy it while he's here. What happens when his job is over though? He'll leave, but will he come back, remember me, or even want to see me again?"

I sighed deeply. "He is so beautiful though, isn't he? I don't know if there has ever been someone that has even come close to him that this town has ever seen.... And I.... yes, little ol' me, just had the best date in the world with him."

I continued to pet Sassy, collecting my thoughts and fighting sleep. She licked her paws and cleaned her face and then within minutes was curled up and purring herself to sleep by her bowl.

"Good idea, Sass," I locked the door and turned off the light. "See you in the morning. I'm going to bed."

I snuggled into bed surrounding myself with extra pillows. As tired as I was I found myself staring at the ceiling rewinding back through the evening. I wondered if James was doing the same thing in his apartment.

Just as I was drifting off to sleep I felt Sassy jump onto the bed. She curled into a small ball by my side and together we fell asleep.

CHAPTER 33

James turned toward his apartment and came face to face with AJ, who was just returning from a late-night trip to the pharmacy for cough medicine. He needed sleep, he explained, and the only thing that helped was narcotic- infused cough reliever.

James wished him a good night, said he hoped he felt better, then unlocked his own door. He walked inside pulling the door closed behind him, and leaned against - a mirror image of Annie's posture in her apartment.

A smile creased his face. He was glad everything had gone so well. He had worried Annie wouldn't like the plans he had made. The fact that she seemed genuinely pleased made him almost giddy.

He wasn't quite ready to go to bed. Instead he headed to the kitchen to find something to eat, not that he was hungry - he just needed to do something besides sit there and wonder if Annie was feeling the same stirrings as he was.

As he pulled out deli turkey from the refrigerator and spread mayonnaise on white bread he thought about his ex-wife.

I never planned a night like this for her, he mused. *But then, she never would have appreciated it even if I had. She was a woman with no imagination, no dreams.*

Why is it different now, he pondered. *Is it just because I'm older? More willing to try? Or is it the company?* He allowed the evening to play over in his mind again.

I really enjoyed being with Annie. She's beautiful, smart, and she has a mind of her own, goals and dreams.

The day you don't have dreams is the day you don't wake up to see daylight, he repeated to himself like a mantra.

At that moment he realized how much he truly hated his job. He realized the reason he worked on the pipeline for so long was solely based on the money. When he got divorced the pipeline gave him a means of running away from his life, and of course the money was still nice.

Now, money wasn't the only thing that mattered in life. Meeting Annie showed him that there were, as sad as the cliché sounded, more fish in the sea.

He plopped down on the sofa, turned on the television to an old western and after picking off the crust, ate the sandwich in three bites. He washed it down with a can of cola, then decided the Duke could handle the bad guys without him. He switched of the TV and headed for bed. The last thing he wanted was for his roommate to come home and start harassing him about the big date.

Lying in bed, staring at the ceiling, he watched the shadows of the branches dance around the room. Unseasonably warm air blew through James' room from the open window. He didn't pull the covers back but simply laced his fingers behind his head and forced his eyes shut. His thoughts drifted into dreams.

He was working in his family's restaurant and as far away from the pipeline as possible. His dream-self was looking into the mirror behind the bar and talking to Annie, who he could just see as a small figure in the corner of the reflection. If he moved too much she disappeared.

She didn't say anything. She just smiled at him. He felt happy. He heard Mark's dad in the background.

Where are all the fish were we are supposed to catch? he asked. Dream James turned around and held up his pole and showed his bass. When he turned back around to face the mirror a message replaced Annie's face.

It read "What a Catch!"

James rolled over on his bed. The dream faded, and he fell into the deepest and best sleep he had since he began work in this town.

CHAPTER 34

In two separate rooms at exactly the same moment two people were waking with smiles on their faces. The time was just after six o'clock and even though one of them didn't need to be at work for another twelve hours she found herself thinking about a guy. The same man was rushing to get in the shower, not so much to get clean but more to wake up.

James had slept so soundly that he didn't hear his alarm go off at five thirty and was now rushing to make it out the door before he was expected on site for work at six thirty.

While the water washed the sleep from his eyes he thought of me though and hoped my night was as restful as his. He didn't know that separated by only four walls I was staring in his direction hoping the day would hurry up and get done so I could see him again.

Finally getting up I looked out the window and hoped to see James and the guys leave. Realizing it was late though I knew it was probably just wishful thinking. It was still somewhat dark outside but I thought I saw the back of the truck disappear in the distance.

Then, I saw the 'Open' sign to the bakery and caught a whiff of fresh donuts. I put on a pot of coffee and threw my hair up in a loose bun. In old cut off sweatpants and my faded "80's Rock Will Never Die" t-shirt I headed out to get a couple warm chocolate frosted donuts for breakfast.

I was back inside before my coffee was done and was able to catch the morning news for the first time in weeks. The weekend was supposed to be just as nice as yesterday was which meant a large turnout was to be expected for the Independence Day event on Sunday.

At eight thirty I called the hospital to check on Pap, and he sounded completely back to normal. The main reason I knew he was getting better was because he was back to complaining about how nothing was getting done in the yard, and his garage was missing him while he wasn't home. You could hear the pain in his laugh as he enjoyed his own joke, but it was nice to know he was improving.

He was more curious to know how my night went, and Gram fought him for the phone to get all the juicy details.

"There is nothing really to tell, except I had a wonderful, wonderful time!" I happily said.

"Nothing to tell?" She asked, surprised.

"Nothing," I replied.

"Nothing? At all?" She continued to probe.

I gave in. "Okay, so we kissed, and held hands, and I'm sure there was a hug or two in there. Happy?"

I heard her relay everything to Aunt Liz, and then Liz try to disguise her excitement and half shouted, "Go girl" while Gram hushed her to be quiet in the hospital.

"Thanks Liz." I blushed.

"Well not to change the subject, because I still want to know more, but as long as things stay the same, and if Pap has his way, he'll be getting out of here tomorrow," Gram noted.

I looked up and said a silent prayer, thanking God, and then commented, "Well you tell him that the town will have fireworks for him when he comes home."

"Ha, Liz said she's taking him to the celebration even if she has to push him around in a wheelchair." Gram chuckled.

"Yeah, but she's not joking," I said. And as I heard the doctor call out his good morning in the background I let them go, asking them to give me a full update if anything changed. It was only fair since they required the same after my date.

I pressed the release on the phone base and dialed Kate at work to make plans for a girl's gossip lunch. As my partner in crime on the "perfect dress hunt" she was probably dying to know how everything went. She excitingly accepted my invitation telling me to meet her at the café at eleven thirty.

Catching me off guard she stopped me from hanging up. "Wait, before you go, I have to know...which did he like better, the dress when it was on you or off?"

The last of my second cup of coffee was now showered across my television screen.

Kate laughed in the background, and before hanging up said, "Just kidding!! See you in a little while, Annie!"

CHAPTER 35

Kate worked as an assistant in the mortgage office at the lone bank in town. As I walked past on my way to the restaurant I waved at her through the window. She acknowledged me by holding up five fingers to indicate she would be there in a few minutes.

I grabbed the last booth by the windows and watched for her to come down the sidewalk. Looking over the handwritten specials on the chalk board I was interrupted with a small tap on the shoulder.

Turning around I saw my grandparents' neighbors Frank and Celia. "How is your pap?" Frank asked.

Before I could answer Frank continued, "You know that man is tougher than anyone I know, and one of the best men on earth. He'll be fine, and just know that we are thinking about him," Celia agreed across the table from him.

I thanked him and hoped he could tell how sincere I truly was for his warm thoughts. I loved living in a small town.

Kate knocked on the window seeing me in the booth, and I waved again as she strolled past and came through the swinging door.

"There is the love bird," Kate said, falling into the booth seat.

"You really aren't funny," I teased.

"Yes I am, no need to deny the obvious," she joked.

I chuckled. "Ain't that the truth?"

After ordering two sandwich platters and cherry colas I filled her in on everything that happened. Even as the server laid the food in front of us I continued, not leaving out any details. I didn't want to waste reliving how much fun we had together. I even began to feel his hands wrapped around me, and the same goose bumps came back.

She chewed, and drank, and listened to everything I had to say, and when I was finally done I waited for her to say something, anything. I knew Kate didn't have it in her to stay quiet for long. I could tell she was calculating something in her mind, but instead she simply asked, "So, when are you going to see him again? Outside of work that is."

"I don't know. I guess Sunday at the Independence Day celebration. I work tonight and tomorrow."

"Good, I want to meet him. Stalking him at the mall didn't cut it for me," she said, loudly drinking the last of her cola.

"True. Plus, someone has to tell him embarrassing stories about me," I said.

"Now, you're thinking like me!" she exclaimed.

I paid the tab and hugged her. "Have a great day, and don't work too hard."

"Never. See you later tater. You don't work too hard either, but don't stand around drooling over your lover either," she said.

I just shook my head and smiled watching her walk back down the sidewalk. I wished we could have been closer to her in the past, especially when she was going through such a bad relationship. Even though she joked about my one date, I knew she was probably hurting inside wanting the same for herself.

I parked myself on the bench outside of the café and watched people come and go throughout the rest of the day. The warm breeze and shade from the surrounding buildings kept the area cool.

I pulled a small tablet out of my purse and jotted down a few notes of what was needed for starting at the college. I still needed to check on the balance in my bank account and estimate what more was needed to start classes. As the hour approached two o'clock I started back to the apartment.

Passing the bank, I stopped and found myself walking up the steps and through the front door. Dale, the elderly security guard nodded from his perch by the entrance.

"Hey Dale. Great to see you," I said.

Kate had her back toward the windows and didn't see me as I approached the teller waiting line.

A new, young girl who I didn't recognize called me up to her window. I pulled out my savings book and asked to get the balance to date. The magic number the finance manager had told me was etched on my brain. What the girl showed me was still lacking a few hundred dollars. I knew there were almost two months until classes started, and even though payment was due for the fall semester by the end of July I was hoping I would be able to still be allowed to complete registration even if a little short.

I could also still hope for grants and scholarships. But I didn't want to rely on it. I was depressed. I could honestly feel myself begin to cry as I stood in the bank. So as quickly as I could I hurried back to the apartment hoping that I wouldn't see anyone that could read my true expression.

Slamming through my front door, I threw my purse on the bed and collapsed face down on my bed. I covered my head with a pillow and silently cried. As much as I wanted to complete the dream of going back to school, this was the first time I honestly didn't know if it would come true.

CHAPTER 36

I had cried myself to sleep and woke up to my bedside phone ringing. Checking my alarm clock I saw that I had been sleeping for over an hour. I answered, and Gram was on the other end. "Great news Annie! It's confirmed! Pap is being released from the hospital in the morning. The final test results came back and everything was better than expected."

I wiped my eyes with my left thumb and forefinger while propped up on my right elbow. "Wonderful news, Gram. Thank you for calling me. And thank you for waking me up. I must have dozed off, and I need to start getting ready for work."

"Still catching up from last night, huh?" she asked.

I sighed deeply. "I guess."

Gram laughed. "Today is Friday so what's on the menu to take to work?"

I almost forgot. I sat straight up and was wide awake. "Gotta go, Gram. Time's a ticking, and I don't even know what I'm making."

I pressed the release on the phone and threw it back on its cradle. Jumping up from bed I ran down the hall and slid into the kitchen. It was three o'clock and the only thing I would have time to make was hot wings. I had bought a bag of chicken legs and wings and because I had no room in my small freezer put them in the refrigerator. Perfect snack for the bar, and after making them my special way knew they'd be a hit with the town's favorite visitors.

In a large mixing bowl I combined the buffalo sauce, flour paste, and olive oil. With just the right amounts of each ingredient it would stick to the chicken perfectly.

Preheating the oven, I washed and cleaned the chicken. The secret to not letting it dry out was to coat the legs and wings with a little oil, cover with foil, and cook halfway through before saucing them. My mouth watered thinking about how good they'd be.

I ran hot water for a shower and quickly put the chicken in the oven. I had to make up a lot of time lost from my nap.

Fifteen minutes later with a towel on my head and robe tied around my waist I was stirring the hot chicken around in the buffalo sauce mixture. Closing my eyes, I took a deep breath and my stomach growled in response.

I still had an hour before needing to be at work. I made a small salad and finished getting ready. After stealing a few wings for my dinner, I wrapped the rest up to take to work. Sitting on the stool, eating the food was the last few minutes of quiet relaxation I would have for the next ten hours.

Thoughts of James made me hurry my dinner and leave with time to spare. I knew he'd be getting done at the job site just as I was getting to work, but he'd be there as soon as possible.

Joey met me at the door and took the warm pan from my hands. He took deep breath in allowing the hot sauce to fill his nose.

"Mmmmm…You've outdone yourself this week, Annie. These will be gone in minutes," he said, setting them down on the bar. He had plates and napkins out before I even made it to the row of stools.

"Be careful, they've got a kick." I sat down and watched him reach in and grab one from the top.

"Have to make sure they are ok for the guests." He laughed.

"Sure. I understand." I returned the laugh.

He chewed for a few seconds and immediately began his interrogation of the evening before. He asked all the questions a father figure would. Including 'was he a gentleman?' and 'what time did you get in?' I simply played along and gave the vague answers any pseudo daughter would.

"And yes, Daddddd, he even kissed me," I said with sarcasm.

He immediately became embarrassed and the conversation ended as he muttered something under his breath and walked through the swinging doors to the office.

"Works every time," I whispered.

CHAPTER 37

Mickey was the first to arrive. He always knew there was food on Friday and was always where the free food was served. His excited demeanor cut the silence as he blew through the door like a hurricane force wind.

"Something smells deeeelicious!" He exclaimed, practically hurrying toward the pan of chicken.

"Enjoy, Mickey." I handed him a plate.

Joey returned with a folder of papers. He spread out the pages, each one featuring a different truck. There were red ones, blue ones, ones in every size, brand, and price range.

"Annie Lou, I need your help," he said. What a great change in subject from just two minutes before.

"Are you making a picture book of vehicles? These would fall under the truck section," I offered.

"No... I'm thinking of trading in my truck. I want your opinion on which one to get. Kim would just pick a pink one if I asked her opinion," he explained.

"Well pink is nice." I paged through the choices as Mickey ate beside me.

I was partial to black. My mom always said even the cheapest car looked classy in black. Taking the picture of the only black truck from the group I handed it to him. "This is the one."

"Black? Really? Hmm. I never thought I was a black truck kind of guy?" He looked over the advertisement and detailed description of the truck.

"Trust me," I said.

It was now thirty minutes after opening and the next few

customers were finally arriving. I wiped the glasses and prepared for the oncoming rush. It didn't take long on a Friday for the crowd to swarm in.

My thoughts must have been broadcast out to the streets because by seven o'clock the wings were long gone, and there was not an empty seat left in the house. Being a holiday weekend, many out-of-towners and ex-residents were back visiting family.

I knew we'd be busy, and Joey parked himself behind the counter with me instead of hiding in paperwork in his office. His nephew would be there before nine to help out both Friday and Saturday during the busiest times of the weekend. I just hoped we could keep up until he got there.

About twenty after seven I saw James come through the door. My eyes had been like magnets attracted to him because even though I had been facing the register when the door opened I had followed him through the doorway before the bell could even ring. I smiled. He returned it and pointed to a side table by the wall to let me know where he'd be.

Joey held up a beer in his direction and met him at his side of the bar. They talked quietly, and James looked in my direction making me realize what was being said. I continued to serve drinks, trying to ignore the hole being burned into my head by his smiling eyes.

The evening turned to night and time flew by. Just before ten James called me over to let me know he was turning in. There was a man-datory meeting in the morning. I hugged him goodbye, apologizing for not being able to talk to him more and told him to have a good night. I watched him walk out the door into the warm evening air. A tall man entered, brushing his arm and they both acknowledged one another with a nod of apology.

I don't know why, but I thought I saw a shiver of disturbance run through James' body at that moment.

CHAPTER 38

Once he passed James I could see the man stood over six feet, was tanned with a build like an athlete, and wore a polo shirt with khaki shorts. He looked familiar, but as he walked into the sea of plain-clothed average men he quickly became out of place.

He took a seat on a corner stool, and once he caught Joey's attention ordered a shot of whiskey with a coke to chase it. Anthony and I refilled empty beer glasses at the opposite end of the counter, and when I turned back around a few minutes later the stranger was laying a folded twenty-dollar bill beside his two empty glasses and turning to leave.

I walked toward the opposite end of the bar just as the bell told on him for walking out the door.

"Joey, who was that?" I asked as he was clearing the space for the next customer.

He wiped the counter. "That, my dear child, was a good tipper." He laughed, opening the till to deposit the twenty.

"But WHO was that?" I asked again.

"I don't know. Someone who doesn't come in here enough. That's for sure." He laughed again.

I couldn't agree more. Tips like that were extreme rarities. Men looking like that were even rarer. He was just beautiful, and even more so, he looked extremely out of place and uncomfortable. He must have felt the same to have left as quickly as he came.

As the rest of the evening settled down and the crowd began to thin, I completely forgot about the stranger who sat in at the stool to the right.

I was feeling the long night on my legs, and by one o'clock when only one customer remained Joey noticed me hold on to the bar and shift my weight from foot to foot. He told me to go home and get some rest, that he and Anthony would close up.

I didn't need to be told twice and quickly said my goodbyes and grabbed my now washed baking dish and purse.

It was ironic to walk out of work only to make another quick turn and be at home a second later. Right inside the entrance I grabbed my mail on my way upstairs.

As I walked up the seemingly steep stairs to the apartments I had an idea. I laid my dish on the step and took out a piece of paper. I wrote a note to James asking him to stop by after his meeting. I folded the page as I turned the corner to his apartment and wedged it between the doorframe and knob.

After walking through the front door, I threw my mail on the counter, went straight to the bathroom to brush my teeth and wash my face, and was sleeping before my head hit the pillow.

CHAPTER 39

The sound of pounding rain on the window awoke me. A loud crack of thunder made me focus my attention to the partially opened curtains. My arm felt like a ton of dead weight from sleeping on it. I hadn't moved all night. Outside it was a torrential downpour. You couldn't see twenty feet away.

The clock was off, but it was light outside. The power was off from the storm. It was also hot. Without the overhead fan moving air or the window A/C cooling off the room it was like a sauna in the apartment.

This weather system was bound to blow in. It had been too hot for too long. I just hoped it would leave as quickly as it came, so the Independence Day Celebration could go off without a hitch.

Making it into the kitchen the battery-operated wall clock read nine twenty. I had slept in. I hoped James hadn't already tried to come by, and I slept through it.

I pulled on a pair of jean shorts and a tank top and slid my feet into a pair of flip flops. Carrying my makeup to the window to get better light I quickly splashed on my face, topping it off with a generous dab of lip gloss. I threw my hair into a ponytail and headed out the door. I made the two turns around the corner and knocked on the door to the apartment James was staying in. There was no answer. The note was also gone, too. Both situations were good, I hoped.

Back inside the stuffy apartment I opened both windows on the side opposite the wind and rain. I still needed my coffee pick-me-up so I poured the day-old brew into a glass, added ice and milk with some sugar and stirred. Iced coffee was better anyway on this hot and humid morning.

Aiming my arm chair toward the breeze of the window I sorted through my mail. My phone bill was now due, my latest celebrity gossip magazine subscription was expiring, and there was a sale on mattresses at the furniture mart.

Under all the flyers, junk mail and bills was a plain white envelope with a Harrisburg return address. It looked official and coming from the state capital meant that it might be a response to my grant application.

I dropped everything onto the floor but the envelope and sliding my finger under the top quickly opened it. I pulled out the letter. Reading down the page I felt the coffee start to creep back up my throat and I grew cold and dizzy. To calm down I leaned back in the chair.

"We are sorry to inform you that your recent application for grant approval has been denied due to missing information... Social security number was left blank... Reapply next year."

I reread and felt the tears beginning to well in my eyes.

How could I miss the most vital piece of information? I was in such a hurry to send it off by the deadline that I never looked it over again before mailing it.

What would I do now? The same application is what was used for most of the scholarships at the schools. That meant those too would be denied, and I would never be able to afford to start in the fall.

I sat in silence, just staring through the blowing curtains and listening to the rain slow down to a melodic tapping rhythm.

I needed to get out of the now claustrophobic apartment, and I needed to talk to Joey.

CHAPTER 40

I opened the door to a surprised James with his hand mid-knock. "Whoa turbo, where are you off to?" He lowered his arm.

"James! Oh! I'm…I'm sorry, I was going to run to Joey's house for a minute," I wiped my eyes and folded the letter into my hand.

He pointed out the window. "Don't you know it's still raining out there? Anyway, I got your note, but I'll come back in…"

"No. No. Come in!" I opened the door for him.

I apologized for the heat and explained the no power. "Guess we'll just have to find something to talk about."

"Sounds perfect." He entered and wiped his still dripping feet on the entry mat.

I grabbed all the mail into a pile and pushed the chair back to where it was, and then offered him a seat and a drink.

"I also have some donuts," I said, from the kitchen.

"No, I'm fine for now." He sat secretly glancing at the pile of mail on the floor.

"Everything ok?"

I glanced over my shoulder. "Sure. Why?"

"You didn't seem fine. I mean when you answered the door, you were running out like your place was on fire and you looked… well, sad."

Should I lie to him? Make something up? But as I opened my mouth everything came pouring out. I made my way to the couch and plopping down into a gloomy mess told him how the woman at the college told me I owed a certain amount and how I depended on the grant money. I told him how I stopped by the bank and was disappointed when I saw that there was still a major gap. When he

105

saw me at the door I was going to beg Joey for a full seven days of work and anything extra he could find for me to do.

Just as I finished the power came back on. We looked at each other for a few seconds and then laughed as if something that was said was funny.

He grabbed my hand and pulled me up. "Come on. We're getting out of here for a little while. I have something I wanted to do today."

I reluctantly followed knowing I probably looked like the mess that I felt. James continued to hold my hand, and we walked down the stairs and out the door to the freshly washed street.

He led us to the grocery store a couple blocks down and grabbed a basket by the front door. I didn't say anything just went with him up and down each aisle. When we were standing by the checkout I finally asked, "What, may I ask, are you planning?"

"Lunch," he simply replied.

CHAPTER 41

James parked me on a stool and took over my kitchen. I only spoke when he asked me where the pans or olive oil were. As he opened packages and assembled ingredients he told me how his mom would make this dish when he was little and that he would watch just as I was doing learning the steps. Then, one day he made it for her birthday, and she swore she'd never make it again because his was so much better.

As everything sizzled and cooked in the pan and the scents filled the air I realized how hungry I was. I hadn't eaten since the salad and wings from four o'clock the evening before.

With his back toward me I caught myself staring at how with each movement his shoulders stretched the tight t-shirt he was wearing. I began to have other thoughts, and just as I was about to stand up and move closer he turned around with the plate in his hands.

"Tada," he exclaimed. "A Reuben Sandwich."

"A what-wich?" I asked, slinking back onto the stool and making an obvious disgusted face.

"Trust me."

He laid the plate in front of me.

I just looked at the two-toned rye bread and tried to see what was in the middle.

"Corned beef, thousand island dressing, Swiss cheese, and sauerkraut." He answered my unspoken question.

I spun the plate, still staring. "That's an odd combination.... And sauerkraut. Yuck! You know what that is, don't you?" I asked, thinking about the rotting cabbage.

"Yes, and it all goes perfectly together."

I picked up the sandwich examining it one more time and cautiously smelled the side of it. Then, before changing my mind I closed my eyes and took a bite.

James watched me chew for a few seconds and finally swallow. Silently, I took a bigger bite and nodded my approval. It was delicious. Probably the most unusual thing I'd ever eaten but absolutely delicious.

"That is THE perfect sandwich, James," I said, after the second bite.

"I told you to trust me," he said.

He pulled the other stool close to me, and we ate together.

"How was your meeting?" I asked, remembering his reason for leaving early last night.

"Could have been better." He purposely cut the conversation short. He lowered his eyes and shoved the last fourth of the sandwich into his mouth making it impossible to speak.

I didn't pursue the question. He was obviously upset. Maybe the meeting was bad news or didn't go as he hoped.

"Let's watch a movie before I need to get ready for another night of work," I suggested.

I pointed him to the direction of the videos on the shelf and invited him to pick one out for us. I poured two glasses of cola and popped some popcorn while he pushed play.

When I made it back to the couch I recognized the beginning music of *Love Story*.

"Don't tell the guys, but this is one of my favorite movies," he whispered.

"Your secret is safe with me." I sat down close to his side.

He automatically wrapped his arm around my shoulders and pulled me close.

The movie began, and I threw popcorn into my mouth and sipped my drink. I stared at the screen, but didn't really hear a word from the television.

All my ears could focus on was the sounds coming from the man beside me. The chewing, swallowing, and his heart beating near me. It wasn't distracting, but instead mesmerizing. I found myself wondering what he was thinking, if anything. Or was he engrossed in the movie, ignoring how close we were at that moment?

Twenty minutes later with the popcorn container now empty and on the floor beside me I found my hand move to the edge of my leg and touch his.

I felt him shift in place and I looked up at him and smiled. As if it was a cue to kiss me he did just that. His lips were warm and sweet from his drink. My hand gripped his leg and then moved to his shoulder, and I turned toward him.

The kiss turned deeper, and he pulled me close. It felt as though the tension he was holding in was released through his passion. And I enjoyed every minute, needing the closeness as much as he needed to give it.

The next thing I realized the rain was pounding once again and I was being laid down on the couch. The movie continued to play in the background as James and I made love for the first time. In my living room. On my couch.

It was anything but what I would have planned, but perfect nonetheless. As we held each other in the minutes after, we didn't say a word, just continued to kiss and hold each other. Finally, I had to say what was on my mind. I laid my cheek on his chest and quietly said, "I think I'm falling in love with you."

And then he answered, "I was wondering how long it would take for you to feel the same way I do."

CHAPTER 42

After announcing my need to take a shower and get ready for work James kissed me gently on the lips. "I'll see you in a little while," he said.

I stood under the spray of water and simply smiled replaying the afternoon in my mind. I could hardly contain my excitement and found myself humming and then singing in the shower. I could not remember the last time I was truly this happy. It even made me forget about the delivered bad news from the mail.

I dried off, wrapped my robe around my waist, and then called Gram to check on Pap. They were finally home and he was settled into a makeshift bed on the pull-out couch. Just glad to be home he told me he loved me and to not worry. If he had his way he'd be seeing me at the town festivities tomorrow.

After Gram got back on the phone I told her to take care of the stubborn man and to hide the keys since he might just follow through on his promise about tomorrow.

As I was saying goodbye there was a light knock on the door. Standing in the kitchen in just my robe I hesitated and pulled it closed at the neck.

"Who is it?" I asked.

"Just me," James said.

I peeked my head out the door and he said, "Missed you already... Just couldn't wait to see you later." Then, he kissed me.

I let go of the door and allowed him to push it open with his shoulder while still kissing me and walking into the apartment.

James shut the door with his foot and walked me backwards to the bedroom. He pulled my towel from my wet hair, and at the foot of the bed untied the robe and it dropped to the floor.

I hurriedly pulled his t-shirt off and unzipped his pants. They fell off as he lay back with me on the bed, never releasing the original kiss he had planted on me at the door.

I closed my eyes and enjoyed the moment. He held me tight and enveloped my entire body the entire time. It was as if we were molded together. A perfect fit. How could I ever let him go?

As we lay facing the window he whispered his love into my hair, and I snuggled close to him. We stayed in that position until the clock read that I only had fifteen minutes before the bar opened.

Closing the bathroom door, I asked James to wait for me while I got ready.

I threw on my clothes, blew my hair dry and twisted it up into a clip. In less than two minutes I had quickly put on my makeup and sprayed on my perfume. Once again, I had the same smile plastered onto my face.

I slipped my shoes on and walked out into the kitchen area. James was sitting on the stool drinking water, and he smiled when he saw me.

"You look more beautiful than I've ever seen you," he said.

"Thank you." I winked at him and then I suggested, "Now, what do you say we leave together. Maybe you can even walk me to work."

CHAPTER 43

Laughing, James and I walked into the bar hand in hand Joey looked up from the invoices he was working on and furrowed his eyebrows in question. Then, just as quickly, he looked back down and secretly smiled.

"What can I get ya?" I asked James as I took my post behind the counter.

"Nothing on tap," he whispered.

I laughed and poured myself a cola.

"Hey, listen, I'm going to take a shower and do some laundry. I'll stop by later to see you." He walked around the corner and pecked me on the cheek.

He raised his hand and nodded once as if to say goodbye.

Joey interrupted my staring at James to ask how my Pap was doing now that he was home. I filled him in on everything I knew. Then, as if he couldn't contain his curiosity anymore, he asked about James and me.

"You know I think you more than anyone deserves to be happy. And you seem very happy. But he better not hurt you..." He started down the father-figure road.

"Joey, he hasn't hurt me. In fact, he's...he's perfect," I answered shyly.

Before he could continue his warning on what would happen if he did anything to hurt me I reached over and hugged him.

"Thank you for caring about me, Joey. I love you, too," I said.

"That's good, because I have something for you," he said. "Be right back."

I started cutting limes when Joey came back with a small bag. He handed it to me, and said, "Happy early birthday."

"Early? You're right about that. You're almost a month early," I said, slowly looking in the bag.

A small rectangular shaped box sat at the bottom of the brown gift bag. I reached in and took it out shaking the box. It was pretty heavy for the size.

Opening the top, I could see a set of keys in the box. I tilted my head slightly, thinking of what they were for.

As if to answer me Joey said, "I didn't trade the truck, Annie. I kept her for you. You've done so much for me here, and I'm so proud of you going back to school. You'll need a way to get there. Plus, we just want you to have it."

I didn't know what to say. It was overwhelming. I was elated. Shocked. Surprised. Then, I started crying. I didn't even know tears were falling until the warm drops hit my hands.

"What's wrong, Annie?" Joey asked, coming to my side.

"Thank you so much," I finally said. "You have no idea how much this means to me, Joey." I turned and hugged him again.

"Are you sure you're ok?"

I nodded but finally told him about the dilemma that came up that morning with the mail. "I just hope I'll be able to even go to college," I said.

"Oh sweetie, of course you will. Don't worry. I have faith that everything will work out, and of course I'll do anything that I can for you," he said. "Now, go look at your new truck."

I grabbed the box with the keys and practically skipped out the door. In the farthest spot to the right of the building there sat Joey's silver ten-year-old truck. It was glistening from him washing it right before parking it there. I opened the driver's door and climbed in. Kim had tied a bow to the steering wheel and added a handmade gift tag with the word "Congratulations." She had signed it "Love, Joey and Kim."

"You can even keep it parked right here." He pointed in front of the truck. An "employee of the month" sign was tacked to the fence behind the sidewalk.

I chuckled and once again hugged Joey. I was so happy at the moment. I couldn't wait to tell James as soon as I saw him again.

CHAPTER 44

The bar was even busier than the night before. There were more new faces that showed up, usually dragged in by a regular they were staying with for the holiday weekend. Mickey even brought his uncle and cousins in for a short visit. It was the quickest I had ever seen him come and leave since I started working there.

Just as I was falling into my routine of mixing, filling, and washing a figure coming into the door caught my eye. He was the tall, handsome stranger from the night before. This time he was with my friend Kate. And now my curiosity went through the roof. They crossed in front of the bar and straddled stools at the far side. They were in deep conversation, and I didn't waste a second. I walked right up and interrupted them.

"Hey girl, what can I get you… guys?" I paused between words.

She looked up. "Annie! Long time no see. I want an Amaretto Sour."

"And same for me," the stranger looked up and answered.

I was mesmerized. He was so familiar, and his eyes were a deep, rich brown that held my gaze for a moment too long.

Finally, I broke my stare and made the drinks.

"Here you go, guys." I set the glasses down in front of them.

I bit my lip, wondering how to ask the most obvious question of who Kate drug in when she answered for me. "You remember my older brother Evan, right?"

Her brother? The person I remembered had gone off to school on the other side of the state years before. I remembered him being overweight, out of style, and battling a mild case of acne. This was not the same Evan.

He read my shock. "Yes, Annie, you were the girl who would sneak

114

scary movies into the house with my sister, and we'd watch them when my parents were in bed. Then, they'd force us to get up and eat an early breakfast, and we'd be miserable all day. Look at you… you look so different, so grown up!"

"Me? Evan, you are a completely different person!" I exclaimed.

"Yeah, I think I left half of myself back at college." He chuckled.

We all laughed together, and I promised them we'd get together sometime at the town celebration the next day.

By nine o'clock the place was standing room only. As I made my way down the bar taking orders and making small talk I finally came to the far side. A hand reached through the crowd across the bar. A single rose was balanced on the edge. I smiled when I saw it was James who laid it there.

He was surrounded by his coworkers, who made some snide remarks, as men do. To add fuel to the fire I walked around to the other side and threw my arms around his neck and gave him the biggest, deepest kiss I could. The catcalls got louder, and Vince pulled out his camera and took a picture.

I walked back around to pick up where I left off and didn't say a word. I heard the camera being wound and the flash going off again. I looked up while smelling my rose just in time to be caught in the light.

"Okay, Vince, what are you doing?" I had to ask.

"Just taking some pictures to show my boys what their dad's been doin," he answered by flashing another picture.

I shielded my eyes. "Save the film for the fireworks tomorrow."

Then I looked at James and mouthed a quiet, thank you for the gift.

He answered with a simple wink, and then turned to hang out with his friends.

CHAPTER 45

At one forty I announced final call. It was ten minutes later than usual, but the bar was still very crowded, and one thirty had come and gone as my hands rushed to wash glasses and keep pace with my nightly clean up.

With the news that it was so late many patrons decided to just cash out and leave. James had stayed the entire time. He was only drinking water and chatting with those sitting closest to him. Most of his coworkers were long gone. I was excited he chose to stay.

When the last two guests left at 1:56 he quickly locked the door behind them and came around the bar to help me finish up.

I told him that most of the actual cleaning was done the following morning by Anthony. He earned most of his pay by restocking supplies and physically scrubbing the floors and bathrooms.

With his help putting away the dishes I was ready to leave by ten after the hour. I peeked in to Joey's office and urged him to hurry up. It was late, and morning would be coming soon. He agreed and piled the money he was counting into the safe. There was always another day to do the office work. As grand marshal of this year's celebration, he had to be there when everything began.

By nine o'clock in the morning the streets would start to be filled with vendors. The visitors would then start mingling around about an hour later. It was such a tradition that I could set my clock to it.

My night though was just starting. I had to make my four-time award winning apple pie for the baking contest. Judging would be eleven o'clock so I had to make sure it was done before crashing for the night.

When James walked me to my door I hesitated with my hand on

the knob. If I invited him in I wouldn't want to bake. Other items would be on my agenda. I blushed at the thought.

"What's wrong?" he asked.

Then, I had an idea. "How would you like to help me bake a pie?

"Tonight? Now? I mean. I can. Sure." He stumbled, confused.

I told him my dilemma, and he agreed to peel the apples. I didn't tell him but that was my least favorite part.

After cutting up apples, rolling dough and throwing flour at each other we assembled the pie into a picture-perfect masterpiece. I slid it into the oven and set the timer. As I turned around James was waiting with another handful of flour. It hit my mouth just as I was about to tell him thank you. I coughed and gagged and blindly walked to the sink. Splashing water on my face, I started laughing uncontrollably.

James, who was quiet behind me because he had thought it went into my eyes relaxed and laughed to. He grabbed me and pulled me into his arms and held me tight while planting a kiss onto my dripping lips. I hadn't even had time to dry off my face. He didn't care. I didn't either.

I led him to my bed and let him take off my clothes once again. Together we knew exactly the steps to take to get naked. Before anything else happened, he stared into my eyes and professed his love for me. He sounded sad when he said it, and I quickly told him I loved him too, and seconds later we were engrossed in utter passion. There was nothing more perfect that that moment.

My mind went blank and I could only conjure up one thought: I could get used to this.

We lay in each other's arms, and while James had his eyes closed I was staring at the ceiling fan above us. With each rotation I was hypnotized into a deeper dream-like state. In my mind I could see our future. I could see a beautiful wedding, the two of us traveling and talking about a family.

I was awakened by the timer going off in the kitchen. I didn't know if it had been a dream or my imagination, but I hurried to take the pie out so I could get back to my thoughts before they had time to even think about disappearing.

CHAPTER 46

I slept so soundly that I didn't even move the entire night. Sometime that morning James had left because when my alarm went off I woke up staring at a piece of paper that simply read 'I'll see you soon'. It was signed with a heart and a messy 'J'. It made me smile.

After taking a long warm shower, I took the time to put two braided ponytails down my back and adding red, white, and blue ribbons to the ends. My navy shirt had white ruffles and I paired it with a red tennis skirt. Four years before I hand- crafted my flip flops by adding strips of tied patriotic colored fabric.

This is the one day a year I can pull them out of the bottom of the closet. I looked in the mirror and debated taking my hair down and changing clothes because I resembled a second grader, but I didn't care. I had waited three hundred sixty-four days to dress like this. It was finally the Fourth of July.

I looked out the window and saw the street vendors lining up. A makeshift stage from a tractor trailer was parked in the lot across the street and music was being pumped through the speakers erected on either side of bleachers. The day would be filled with every type of music. Local bands playing everything from Bluegrass to Motown would have their time under the sun today. And the stage would remain full until after the fireworks that evening. Across the street and on the other side of the bakery picnic tables were set up for the food vendors.

After dropping my pie off at the judging stand I took a walk around watching everyone set up. Some older residents sat on lawn chairs or on benches and talked over coffee. That reminded me that I should probably find breakfast before it got busy. I settled on a frozen chocolate banana and vanilla milkshake from the dairy cart, one of the few vendors completely set up and ready for business.

I guess a frozen chocolate banana counted as breakfast because it did have fruit it in. And the milkshake was made with real whole milk. Regardless, it tasted good on this warm morning. I ate as I walked around hoping to run into James. I wondered where he ran off to, and when he intended to come back.

I was scheduled to man the cash register at the Women's social committee cakes and candy stand during lunch, and would be in charge of face painting for two hours in the afternoon. Then I was free to enjoy the rest of the day. Rides, animals, and entertainers were brought in for the special occasion, and people literally covered the entire town.

No matter what day the Fourth fell on, the town automatically switched to celebration mode. Stores and restaurants celebrated the day with open doors and special sales, at least during daylight hours. But when it was time for the fireworks to start, every business in town closed. A banner was hung on either end of town and windows and poles throughout area were decorated with balloons, ribbons, or signs. It really was a sight to see.

About an hour into my cashier job I heard a familiar chuckle from the sidewalk. Looking up while counting change back for a customer I saw Kate's brother walking toward me. He seemed to have been glowing with confidence and once he got closer I caught of whiff of it to from the cologne he was wearing.

"Annie!" he exclaimed, and reached out giving me an awkward hug.

I waited for him to continue. When he didn't I asked him how he was enjoying the day and how his visit with the family was going.

"Very good! I really miss this place. Chicago is nice, just a little bigger… And busier," he joked.

"Yes, that it is," I said. "What are you doing in Chicago?"

"Real estate. I like it, keeps me busy… like the city." He laughed at his own pun.

I simply smiled, and looking over his shoulder saw a small crowd forming. "Well, hopefully I will run into you later, Evan."

"Me too," he said. It sounded like he was implying more.

All I could think was how different we both were from the many years before when we knew each other an entire lifetime ago.

CHAPTER 47

I stood in front of the line of pies the judges had sampled. Each one had a missing piece that had been divided among five judges. There were fruit pies, cream pies, even pies that I couldn't tell whether they were cream or fruit. Over thirty pies sat side by side, and as I looked from one to the other I felt even more confident that my apple pie had a good chance to win.

It was one thirty and the town knew that it was time for the annual winner to be announced. Because of that a large crowd had gathered under the tent and were staring with anticipation, just as I was.

Mayor Thompson took his place on a makeshift podium. He had a notecard in one hand and megaphone in the other.

"Welcome everyone to the twenty second annual pie baking contest at our wonderful town Independence Day celebration." He swung his hand holding the card around to show the area and spoke loudly into the megaphone.

The crowd clapped, and he quickly continued with the explanation of the results. "As in the past judging went through three rounds with a final decision of first, second, and third place winners. We have had more participants this year than ever, and speaking for the judges must say this was the hardest one yet to judge."

He readjusted the card and focused his eyes on the small writing. "And now the moment you've all been waiting for. Third place and winner of a trophy and fifty dollars savings bond is.... Marian Schultz with her chocolate cream pie."

There were cheers from the left, and Marian smiled and clapped as she walked toward the Mayor. His assistant handed her the trophy and envelope, and he shook her hand.

Before she made it back to her spot he spoke again. "On to second place…Oh, it's a familiar one here. Congratulations to…. Annie Blackwell and her apple pie. She will take home a trophy as well and a one-hundred-dollar savings bond."

Louder applause erupted as I realized my name was just called and headed to the table. I quickly accepted my award and almost embarrassed walked back to my spot.

Mayor Thompson continued. "Now, for first place. Wow, it's a new contender. Well, that's just fabulous! Please help me in congratulating James Murphy and his Strawberry pie! He will take home this magnificent trophy and a two hundred fifty-dollar savings bond."

I was stunned and then elated. As I watched him come into my peripheral vision to my right I could see a familiar head of red hair bounce into the room. His face was red with embarrassment, and his eyes showed surprise. I realized I had my hands over my mouth, and then I started cheering and whistling. The crowd joined in. He shook the mayor's hand and accepted his envelope and then walked in my direction. I hugged him and kissed his cheek.

"I had no idea that you baked too," I said. "So that's what you went off to do."

"Yeah, I just like making food. Sorry I beat you though." He innocently apologized.

"Well, because it's you I guess it's okay." I laughed.

After the awards were given out the pies were sliced and pieces were sold for donation. I pulled James to the front table. "I want a piece of your award-winning pie before it's all gone. I need to know why yours beat mine."

"Yours, too," he said. "I technically helped make the first and second place pie."

We sat at a picnic table under a shade tree and each ate the other's pie in silence.

As each of us took the last bite I spoke first, "That definitely was worthy of first place."

"Too bad I don't like strawberries," he said, laughing.

I playfully hit his arm, and he gripped my hand and led me down the sidewalk.

CHAPTER 48

The rest of the afternoon was perfect. We spent the entire time together. He sat and watched me paint children's faces, we visited the antique car show, and we even rode the Ferris wheel. James followed wherever I directed him, only complaining once, and that was when I rushed him away from a '67 Chevy he fell in love with. At six o'clock we had corn dogs and shared a large basket of homemade French fries for dinner. We were listening to a bluegrass band and people watching. Some local elders of the community were square dancing with each other. James watched in fascination.

"I want to be able to do that when I'm their age," he said, noting their energy as they twirled their partners around.

"What are you talking about? I want to be able to do that now." I chuckled.

"Touché," he agreed.

As we were looking for the perfect place to watch the fireworks show we passed by Gram, Pap, and Liz. Gram sat on a lawn chair beside Pap who was in a wheel chair. Liz was on a blanket beside him. She squealed with delight when she saw me.

"Come here, you two. We were hoping to see you, and I saved you guys a seat." She patted the blanket beside her.

"What are you doing here?" I asked them as a group but was looking at Pap.

"I told you I wouldn't miss this," he answered, opening his arms for a hug.

I embraced him and then hugged Gram and Liz, too. James shook Pap's hand and told him how great it was to see all of them again.

We took them up on their offer, and I made small talk until the sun fell behind the horizon, and the music turned into a patriotic tribute from the local high school marching band.

I noticed then that the closer I got to James the quieter he got. He stayed beside me. He continued to hold my hand. But he didn't say more than a few sentences for the rest of the night.

It could have been that he was concentrating on the sounds of the fireworks or because the patriotic songs from the band on stage. At ten o'clock when the day's celebration was coming to a close Liz wheeled Pap down the sidewalk as we said goodbye.

James and I walked home hand in hand, and once again it was eerily quiet. I knew he had been up early making his award-winning pie, so I assumed that was the reason he was quiet.

When we got to my apartment door and put the key into the lock James finally spoke.

"I had a wonderful day, Annie. I hope you did, too." He pulled me to face him.

"I did. It was perfect," I replied.

"I'm going to leave you to rest. I have a long day tomorrow," he said quietly.

"Ok. I understand." I kissed him goodnight. Then, seconds later I was in my apartment, and James was on his way to his.

CHAPTER 49

James held a secret. It ate away at his stomach and even though he didn't have a final answer to a question that was haunting him he nonetheless held the uneasiness in each breath he took.

He wondered if Annie could read the stress. He wanted to pull her aside tonight and tell her what was bothering him, but without a definite answer he knew it would only cause her to be upset.

He would know more tomorrow when he met with his boss one final time. He had enough time to carry out a plan he knew needed to be done. And then, regardless of what happened after tomorrow he would feel okay. He knew they'd be fine. For now, he lay on top of his covers with his hands behind his head, and he stared at the ceiling. He knew that no matter how tired he was his nerves would keep him up that night.

After an hour of watching the moonlight dance on the ceiling and not feeling the least bit like sleeping, he knew the only way he could welcome sleep was to empty the thoughts in his head. Turning on the light on his night stand he took a piece of paper and wrote a note. He wanted to put his feelings on paper in case he needed to use it later.

Forty-five minutes later he turned off the light and rolled over onto his left side. He stared out the window for thirty seconds and then shut his eyes and was easily asleep in no time.

~

Across the building I too was fighting sleep. I lay awake and wondered why James was so quiet. Had we gotten too close too fast? Did he regret his decision to be with me? I realized I shouldn't overreact, that it was crazy to assume the worst when he was probably just tired as he said he was.

Regardless, it bothered me enough to turn on the side table lamp and pull out my romance novel that I used to help fall asleep. Four chapters later I finally felt my eyelids get heavy, and I shut off the light, turned on my side, and within a few seconds my questions were forgotten and I was finally asleep.

~

What felt like ten minutes later I opened my eyes but immediately knew I didn't feel right. The sun was just coming up and so was last evening's funnel cake and corndog.

I made it to the bathroom just in time. It had been a long time, and I prided myself on never getting sick, but there was no denying it. I had some type of stomach bug.

And I was exhausted. Even though I had slept a while it felt like I was just getting ready to crawl into bed for the night. I pulled the curtains closed and sank deep into the covers of the bed. To top it off I covered my head with a pillow and drifted back to sleep.

Six hours later I was awake again and stared at the alarm clock. I had no energy to get out of bed. In fact, the thought of getting up made the nausea return. I knew I had to work that day and missing work meant no money, which also put my school bill even further out of reach.

After another forty minutes I finally found enough strength to drag myself to the kitchen. I opened the coffee container and then heaved it into the trash can. I decided to stick with ice water.

I put my hand to my forehead but didn't feel feverish. I hoped whatever this was that it only lasted twenty-four hours. I actually hoped it was more like a twelve-hour bug or just bad food from the night before and would be gone by the time work started. I always worried about food from a street vendor.

Wrapped in a blanket I watched an old movie on the couch, and as it ended I decided a shower would make me feel better. I headed to the bathroom. I had not gotten sick since that morning, but I had only eaten two pieces of toast and a handful of oyster crackers. I had no appetite, but at least I kept it down.

The shower helped. I finally felt better and assumed whatever it was would soon be gone.

I was wrong.

CHAPTER 50

Work was busy. Most of those visitors that had been in town for the night before were hanging around, at least for another day.

I noticed Evan had come in early, and it wasn't until a few hours later that Kate showed up to sit beside him.

In the time while he was there alone he had kept me entertained with stories of what he'd been up to. After an hour of him distracting me though, I began to ignore most of what he said in an effort to get the orders right that were being yelled toward me from neighboring guests.

By ten o'clock I was exhausted. I knew I was already pushing myself because of the virus I obviously had. Joey noticed too and pulled me into his office.

"If you're not feeling well go home. We will survive and this place will not go anywhere," he said.

"I'm fine. Just tired, but I need the money so I'm staying."

He simply shook his head once and said okay.

When I left the office, I saw Kate waving from the end of the bar. I got her "special drink" ready, and after walking halfway to her slid the glass down into her waiting hand. We both laughed.

"'Bout time you show up," I teased her.

"Hey, this big gal had a big date," she teased back.

"What? Really?" I asked. I knew she had talked about a certain customer at the bank that kept coming to visit her with daily questions on loans.

"Yes, really! Don't be so surprised. We need lovin', too." She made a big hourglass shape with her hands and took a big sip from her stirring straw.

Evan pretended not to hear her, but couldn't help but look down and chuckle too. "So, I take it you had a good time."

"As a matter of fact, you two, I had a great t…" She suddenly stopped and looked up at the door smiling.

I looked over my shoulder and saw Scotty and Will, two of the pipeline workers, walk through the door.

Turning back around, I saw Kate still smiling and looking embarrassed. I looked at the guys and back to Kate.

"Scotty?" I asked.

"No," she simply answered.

"You and…Will? Really?" I was shocked.

"Again, why the surprise, Annie?"

"I'm, I'm just so happy for you, Kate."

I was called to the other side of the bar, and I mouthed back to her that I wanted the details later. She shook her head no with a sly look like she would go to the grave with her secrets. I knew better. After a few more drinks she would be pouring information.

The rest of the night slowly quieted down as my energy left me entirely. Kate and Evan, as well as the pipeline workers, all slipped out while I was cleaning up. Close to eleven o'clock there were only a few more customers, and Joey pointed to the door and told me to go home and get some rest. This time I didn't argue. I welcomed the bed when I lay down, fully clothed, including shoes.

When I roused around two a.m. I kicked off my shoes and climbed under the covers.

I didn't move until morning.

CHAPTER 51

I woke up nauseated. I didn't get sick this morning, so that was good, but I didn't feel well at all. I was able to eat a bowl of cereal, and I decided to try my sister on the phone. It had been a while since I talked to her, and I knew they would soon be relocating back to the states. I was anxious to see her again.

She answered on the third ring. I could tell she was distracted, and she explained that they were informed they would be moving within the next month. She was trying to get things in order. Keeping the conversation short I told her I love her and to call me soon, if only to say hello. She agreed, and then I was left to talk to Sassy about the flu bug I had. She didn't seem interested and jumped off my lap and wandered to the kitchen to eat. Even she had an appetite.

I was staring out my living room window when there was a knock on my door an hour later. I wasn't expecting anyone, and I unconsciously ran my fingers through my hair. I had not yet got dressed and still had the clothes I wore the evening before.

When I unlocked the chain lock from the door and slowly pulled it open. Standing there, half smiling was James. He oddly looked sad and excited at the same time. I was happy to see him but surprised that he was here on a Tuesday morning.

"Hey there. It's good to see you. What a surprise!" I reached up and hugged his neck.

He hugged back, but his grip was lighter than usual. "Hey to you, too."

"What's wrong?" I asked.

He paused as if not wanting to tell me what was going on. It seemed like a lifetime, and then I instantly got a bad feeling. "James?" I provoked again.

He sighed deeply and tried to smile to calm me down. "I need to talk to you, to tell you something."

I became light-headed and didn't know if it was from the sickness or James' impending news. I had to sit down, and I pulled him toward the couch.

I quietly sat and waited. It didn't take him long to get his composure and began by telling me about the meeting he was called to Saturday morning.

"Apparently the site manager for the pipeline crew located in Tulsa was in an accident last week and has been in the hospital. My boss nominated me to take over," he began.

I just looked at him and waited for him to continue.

"I don't want to do it, Annie. But I can't say no. I mean. You know I'm not happy with the pipeline... I would quit in a minute... but I don't have anywhere else to go. I need the job and.... And the money they are offering is too good to be true." He suddenly stopped.

"I understand. No, I completely agree. You should do it. They need you," I quietly said back.

"Really? You understand?"

I just sat there and looked at him blinking. He knew I was lying, that I really didn't understand.

I just chewed on my lips and stared at my hands. I was upset. Or was it anger? I didn't want to talk but knew I had to say something in reaction to what he just told me.

"I thought things were going well. I thought you... loved me... that we would last forever," I said, beginning to feel the tears form in the corners of my eyes.

"I did. I do, I mean. Me leaving doesn't mean we can't be together."

Sarcastically I laughed. "Long distance relationships never work out. You won't be coming back. You know it."

He swallowed hard. "I knew you'd be mad."

I shook my head. "I'm just sad. I knew you'd eventually leave me. Your work wasn't here forever. I just thought it might be different... I thought..."

Then I changed directions, refusing to wallow in pity. "Well, when do you leave?"

He whispered, "They just told me this morning when I showed up on site. They told me I was flying out tonight."

"Tonight? You're serious?" I got up and walked to the kitchen. I didn't know what to do with myself, or how to react. I was devastated. Ten minutes before I was fine. Now my world was turning into a roller coaster. And I wanted to get off.

He came over and put his hand on my shoulder. "But I had to do something for you. I had to make it better, to make you understand that I really do care about you."

I turned around and waited. I couldn't even make eye contact because I knew I would start crying.

"I paid for your school. So you will be okay. You will have enough money for your classes and your books.

This time I looked up at him. "You did what?"

"I put enough in your bank account so you will be able to go to school this fall."

"I don't need your money. I don't need your handout. I just needed you," I said, and now the tears fell, steadily clouding my vision.

I was getting more and more angry. "Just go. Have a safe trip. I hope to see you again. But best of luck if not." I opened the door and motioned for him to leave.

He leaned in and kissed my forehead, and again told me he loved me. Then, the last I heard of him before he left was his footsteps disappear around the corner to his apartment.

CHAPTER 52

It had been almost two weeks since I saw or talked to James. I spent the first week walking around in a daze waiting for him to call or word to come back through his friends. They heard nothing.

I didn't talk to anyone and simply went through the motions at work.

By now Joey knew not to ask me what was wrong. I went to work but didn't put forth any more effort than was required.

On Monday night, thirteen days after he walked out the door I realized I may never see James again. I had to give a message to someone that might speak to him. I was determined to do it now, and then maybe I could sleep, if not breathe again. At ten after twelve I knocked on Vince's door. I knew I would wake him up, but it may be my last chance.

He was squinting when he opened the door. He was tying a robe over his pajamas and his hair stood on end like his fingers were just in a light socket.

"Annie! Are you ok, dear?" He instantly woke up.

I nodded. "I just need…do you know where I could find him? I need to get in touch with him."

"I truly wish I did, hon. Like the others said too, we only had his name and where he was from. He was pretty quiet around us. When we get back home next week I'll see what I can do for you," he said with sincerity.

"I know you will. Can you give him this? If you see or hear from him?" I handed him a sealed envelope.

He slowly took it from my hand. "You know I will."

I said thank you and apologized for waking him. Then, I turned and walked away.

133

That night as I lay in bed my dreams took me back to when I was in Kindergarten.

It was winter and I had on a hat and gloves my grandma knitted for me. As I left the house to get on the bus I noticed it was hot outside. The kids were laughing through open windows of the bus when they saw the way I was dressed.

Turning quickly to run back inside I realized my house disappeared and there was a large sign that said, 'Welcome to Houston'. I tore off my jacket, then my hat and scarf, and turned back to the bus. I could see my reflection in the door and where my blond braided pigtails should have been long red curls blew around my face.

I sat straight up in bed, sweat beading on my forehead. I didn't know why I was so stunned from sleep and tried to force myself to close my eyes. The clock read seven twelve, and this was the exact time when I realized there was no job to go to at the moment, no appointment that I had scheduled, or person I had to meet.

Nonetheless, I was… late.

2000

CHAPTER 53

It was a Monday morning in August, and I couldn't even read the menu at the Donut Drive-up. My eyes were so filled with tears; the more I blinked the more they clouded up.

I settled on two known items, coffee and a plain glazed donut. When I pulled up to the window and held my money out for the cashier she stopped mid-grab.

"You ok, ma'am?" she asked, in her misplaced southern accent.

I nodded, and when I opened my mouth to speak I started crying even harder. The young girl simply handed back my change and order and shut the window.

I wiped my entire face with the napkin from the paper bag and quickly drove away. Just as I pulled out of the parking lot my cell phone rang. It was my sister. I debated whether or not I should answer it. She always questioned what was wrong, no matter how positive I sounded, so I knew she'd be able to tell I'd been crying.

"Hello?" I faked a smile, hoping it would come through on the phone. It didn't.

"Sis, what's wrong?"

"I never thought I would see this day. I'm so sad, yet so happy. I don't know how to act," I explained, instead of lying and telling her nothing was wrong.

When she didn't say anything, I continued. "It's Jamie. She's left me to go to pre-K...pre-K...the step before Kindergarten!" And with that I burst into tears once again. I told her I'd call her later and quickly hung up.

Being the dayshift manager for Marcella's Restaurante, I made the schedule and knew this would be a tough experience, so I took the entire day off. My plans were to stop by the library on the way home, but instead my car took me home.

The first thing I saw was my reflection in the entryway mirror. My red puffy eyes stared back, and I finally laughed. I couldn't imagine what next year would be like. I'd need an entire week when she went to Kindergarten

I took my coffee and donut inside and fell into a kitchen chair. Where had the time gone? A stack of pictures sat on the table with intentions to put them into an album one day.

I took a big bite of donut and picked up the stack. I slowly paged through them thinking back to how this whole journey started.

CHAPTER 54

Simply put: my Independence Day celebration with James made more than just fireworks. That weekend was when my now curly red headed daughter Jamie was conceived.

Nine months later, she was born, and when I saw her red fuzzy head I instantly knew she had to be named after her dad, even if I hadn't seen or talked to him since the day he left.

Don't get me wrong. It wasn't that I didn't try to find him. But 1995 was different than 2000. I didn't have a cell phone, nor did I have the Internet, and I had honestly tried to track him down. I kept in touch with his coworkers, especially Will, who married Kate eighteen months after that Fourth of July weekend. Even after they moved back to Nashville I still wrote to her every week. Then, when I got a computer we emailed every day.

Will just didn't know where he was. He knew James had taken the site manager position in Tulsa, but rumor had it he quit just three weeks later. And he never came back to their headquarters either. When the crew made it home they expected to see James, but his locker was cleaned out. Nobody knew where he went.

I found out I was pregnant two weeks after he left. I knew in my mind it wasn't the flu, but I was so depressed with James leaving that I kept to myself, and never talked to anyone. I didn't tell Joey until I was six weeks along. His reaction was surprising to me. He said he knew--that no mom-to-be ever had such a beautiful glow. He wanted to say congratulations, but knew it probably wasn't a very happy time for me.

After another week of falling further into my depression Joey and his wife invited me and my Gram and Pap to dinner. We talked about everything that needed to be done, and what the future would hold. Everyone agreed this was a blessing, nonetheless, and that everyone would be there to help.

As I was leaving, Joey hugged me and whispered into my ear that my rent was considered free until further notice. As I was about to argue, he gave me a sideways look that I read as "no arguments."

I tried to lead a normal life, to pretend I could handle the changes. I had even started classes at the university that fall. I enjoyed absorbing myself in my studies. It kept me from wondering where James was and what I was going to do with a baby when he or she was finally born – that is until the tuition was due and I received notice of the automatic draft from my checking account.

I guess my dream of the red headed girl at the bus was a prediction of what was to come. At 21 weeks of pregnancy, with Kate by my side we found out I was having a baby girl. I sat in the car staring out the window on the way home and the reality hit me. I would be holding my little girl in a few months. And this was the moment I became excited for the first time.

The picture I held up now was one of Pap holding Jamie in the hospital moments after she was born. You could see me in the background looking to my left staring lovingly at the beautiful little girl in his arms. I knew at that minute that I was head over heels in love with her.

CHAPTER 55

I noted I had a lot of work ahead of me organizing photos since they seemed to be in no particular order. The next three pictures in the series were at her second birthday. It was the before, during, and after shots of her blowing out her Barney cake.

Back then, I could have kicked that purple dinosaur if I ever saw him around town. He occupied over two years' worth of my television face time. I never saw the news, a sitcom or the weather in that timeframe, but I could recite every word and song from the twenty-seven video tapes we had in our Barney Collection.

Now, thinking back, I wouldn't have traded that time for anything, and in fact I'd hug Barney because he taught her so much, from counting and the alphabet, to how to brush her teeth and respect others. And while she danced to his circus and farm tunes I actually was able to clean the house and cook dinner, things you take for granted unless you are a single parent.

The next picture was of her at eighteen months old petting a rabbit at the petting zoo. She had big tear streaks down her face where the goat behind us had rammed his head into the fence scaring her to near death.

The next pictures were a group of ten snow photos from last Christmas. Jamie was playing with Joshua, a neighbor during a big snowstorm. They were making snow angels, digging a cave, and trying to roll a snowball taller than both of them. Joshua's dad came to the rescue and the last picture showed them around the snow man which stood over six feet tall. That night Jamie asked me when she was going to get a dad to help make snowmen.

I had never kept it secret, and she has always known James was her dad. I even said he was probably looking for us. I knew that wasn't entirely true. If it was he would have found us. I had only moved a mile down the road and everyone in town knew where to find me. She accepted that, but when she prayed at night, or played by herself where she didn't know I was listening she would always ask for or talk to "Daddy James."

It hurt me. With each time it cut deeper. After the talk that day she played in the snow I realized I could at least try a date or two, test the waters in the dating pool.

I went on one blind date, and another one arranged through the church social committee. Both were mistakes. Just as I was giving up hope my past walked back into my life once again.

I was bartending at Joey's one weekend during Christmastime, filling in for Tracy, my replacement hired that summer. I had been ringing up sales on the register, and when I turned around Evan was standing with a box of chocolates. I had not seen him in the last three years before. He had been home for his grandma's funeral and spent every night flirting with me at the bar, but I was still in the fantasy world that James was coming back, so I never gave him a chance.

This time, I jumped in with both feet. Eight months later, we were still together. As much as he would like to move in and take it to the next level in his plan, I don't want to expose Jamie to that. If we were meant to live together it would be after we were married, whenever, or should I say, if that ever happened.

Instantly, I felt heartburn coming on and grabbed for the box of antacids I grew accustomed to carry around. This happened all too often now when I start to think about the future and marriage.

I popped two antacids and stared at the photo of Evan and me embracing and smiling for the camera. I noticed that unlike the picture where I was in the hospital smiling at Jamie, this one looked fake and uncomfortable. I chalked it up to a bad day and continued paging through the photos.

CHAPTER 56

Jamie has always been such a happy child. I'm not saying that because I'm her mom. I've seen other children at the grocery store or park deep in the throes of a tantrum. She wasn't one of these. In fact, pushing her in a cart or walking her in a stroller around the park actually calmed her down.

So, needless to say, I've called her gifted since the first sound she cooed out that resembled a word. The next photo verified just that.

It was the Easter play at church, and Jamie was just turning three. Her class was trying to recite an easy song. Just as it was finishing her part was to say, "Jesus has risen," into a microphone. Instead, she told the entire story of Easter. When she was done the entire congregation stood and clapped, and she shyly ran back to me in our pew.

The pastor stood up behind the podium and simply said, "Amen! Looks like she should write my sermons from now on."

In this particular picture she was in midst of her speech, and she even held one hand up to the sky like an evangelist on the Sunday morning television. This is one of the many days that I cried with pure joy.

Her favorite doll's name is Birdie. I'm not sure why she chose that name, but you can't argue with the imagination of a child. That morning as we were leaving for school she clutched Birdie tight and tried to convince me to take her along. Most of the time I was easy to give in. I overcompensated for being the only parent, and I wanted to let her be happy. This was an instance when I knew I had to stand firm and not allow it.

As her bottom lip began to fall, and I knew what was coming next,

I knelt down and formed the same look on my face. "What will I do here all by myself?" I asked.

"What about me? She needs to be with me," she appealed.

"Honey, you'll be too busy making new friends, and Birdie will be lonely. Let her stay here so we can keep each other company," I said.

She reluctantly gave her to me and spouted out strict instructions on how to take care of her. I saluted her in agreement. She was now face-down on the table in a spilled pool of milk from the cereal bowl Jamie used as she hurriedly left the table that morning.

I wiped her face and thought back to the day she joined our family.

Evan relocated back to our home town the weekend he brought the box of chocolates to me at work. He said he wanted to go out with me to celebrate his new job in the city. His sister was now in Nashville, and he didn't care to really see anyone else. I agreed. Mostly curious to see where it would lead.

At the end of the date he walked me to door, and in his left hand he carried a red and white striped gift bag. Being a gentleman, he said goodnight by hugging me and kissing my cheek. As I opened the door he handed me the bag and said he'd call me soon.

When I got inside I told the babysitter goodnight quietly as not to wake Jamie. When she shut the door behind her I peeked in the bag. There was a card that read 'To: Jamie, From: Santa's Elf.' The gift was Birdie. Today was the first day Jamie didn't take her when she left the house.

And so now, I've found myself crying once again.

CHAPTER 57

The second date with Evan was much harder for me. Our conversation over dinner was more personal and thinking about the past was hard enough let alone actually making myself talk about it.

To lighten the mood, he took me to Santa's Village in the city. This was a vendor-sponsored winter carnival that featured a life size snow globe and slides made of ice.

Adults were even able to slide up to the "Ice Bar" for a hot toddy or special alcohol-enhanced coffee. Even in the freezing temperatures I started to warm to the idea that it wasn't so bad dating again.

That night Evan once again said goodnight and respectfully kissed only my cheek. In my eyes he was a true gentleman just for restraining himself from putting me in an awkward position where I had to kiss him back.

I told him I had a wonderful time and invited to make him dinner the next evening. He quickly accepted and turned walking down the sidewalk. At his car, he waved as I opened the front door.

It was just before eleven o'clock, and I knew exactly what I needed to do before putting myself to bed. I ran a hot bath and filled it with bubbles until they poured over the side. I slid into the tub up to my chin and closed my eyes. The only sounds I heard were the popping of the small bubbles and Jamie's deep breathing in the next room. It should have been the ideal moment.

Instead my mind swam with thoughts from that evening and they mixed with questions on what would come and what to do. I couldn't relax and enjoy the bath.

I turned on my CD player and listened to soft rock to drown everything out. I didn't hear the phone ring five minutes later. Because my answering machine features the prerecorded man's voice asking to leave a message, the caller didn't leave a message.

This wasn't the first time he had tried to get in touch with me, but it was the last in his mind. He realized before making this call that if I didn't answer he would have to give up. He would assume he either had the wrong number again or that I had obviously moved on with my life and put him in the past.

I quickly peeled off my earphones and listened. I thought I heard something. When all remained quiet I lowered myself even further into the warm water and took a deep breath. I smiled because I felt like everything was going to work itself out.

Now, my mind finally cleared, and I found myself more relaxed than I had for a long time. This time Jamie's breathing drew me toward her room and I found myself missing her even though she was less than twenty feet away. I couldn't get dressed fast enough. After covering her up and kissing her on the forehead, I pulled the rocking chair to her bed and sat there for the next hour just watching her sleep. What a wonderful life I have.

CHAPTER 58

Kate was ecstatic that I was dating Evan. She would ask for details every time we talked on the phone, and my answer would always be the same. "It's my secret to keep. Make some of your own."

Will had found a successful career on Music Row in Nashville and was a sought-after songwriter for some of the biggest names. Everyone liked his young ideas, and they soon were living the dream life in the country music capital of the world. Kate quit the finance scene.

She spent her days mostly volunteering at the nursing home. The day I told her we were officially a couple was in January, and she had actually called to share her own good news. At that time, she and Will had a baby boy named Colby, and she was going to reveal they were expecting again.

Announcing my relationship with Evan changed the balance of the conversation. She had actually squealed with delight. Knowing she obviously approved helped make the decision of finally having a true committed relationship easier. I don't know if I needed her approval or just her support, but she boosted my excitement.

Jamie enjoyed having Evan around. He spent most of his free time at our house, cooking us dinner, watching movies, and even playing dolls and being suckered into a true dress up tea party with Jamie. It wouldn't be until months later that I allowed him to spend the night.

When that night finally did happen I was so excited, and yet a complete nervous and uncomfortable wreck. I fumbled with the bedding and couldn't find the right satin nightgown that I had put aside just for this occasion. In the end we quickly made love and fell asleep with no frills or fancy moments. It was actually rather boring, but satisfying. It wasn't until the next morning that I realized we never even told each other good night.

I made coffee, pancakes, eggs, and bacon. It just felt like the right thing to do, or the very least I could do to occupy my hands. I actually felt embarrassed, which was odd since we dated and spent almost every waking, non-working hour together. But being with Evan was nothing like being with James.

Evan scared me when he walked up behind me and kissed my neck as I flipped pancakes. I jumped, and he stood back and fastened his belt on his jeans. I stood there looking at his firm abs and tan torso. He certainly was good looking. I hugged his neck with the spatula still in hand. "Good morning."

"Sorry I scared you, dear." He hugged me back and then quickly grabbed my rear.

I pretended to hit him with the greasy utensil, and he took off back to the bedroom laughing.

That day, I had to go into work and Evan would watch Jamie. He said he enjoyed spending the time with her, but I knew even on her best behavior the eight hours with her could be extremely exhausting.

Usually, when he watched her they would eat lunch at the restaurant where I worked. I'd get to see her, and she would be proud to be eating at Mommy's job.

Today was no exception. At noon, on the nose, Evan and Jamie walked in and waved from the hostess stand. I whispered to the host to seat them in the small table at the back corner. From there I would be able to sit with them when the lunch crowd calmed down.

I brought her a grilled cheese sandwich cut into four triangles with no crusts and extra pickles just as she always asked for. After she ate everything she was rewarded with a chocolate pudding with whipped cream and two cherries on top, one for me, and one for her.

By one o'clock the lunch rush was all but gone, and I sat down beside her and helped her finish the picture she was coloring. It was her nap time and I said my goodbyes and told her I'd see her soon.

I kissed her on the head and Evan on the cheek. He winked and the two of them were gone seconds later. I sank back into the seat I just got up from and finished off the rest of the chocolate pudding.

I folded up the picture, which was of three lopsided hearts with faces in each. There were two with long hair, one blond, one red haired and one boy with short dark hair. As I looked closer there was the beginning of a fourth heart on the bottom. She had to leave before she finished it. I wonder whose face would have been in that one. I kept all her drawings and this one wouldn't be an exception, so I put it in my apron for safekeeping.

CHAPTER 59

Somehow, this folded picture became mixed in with the photos I was going through that August day. I unfolded and added it to the refrigerator art that covered the front and sides of the black appliance.

I put it beside a picture she just drew last month. We had come back from a week at the beach. She liked to put red or yellow – as she called blonde - hair on everyone. This time the three people in the picture were standing on the sand by the ocean and one held a shovel, one what looks like a kite, and the third one oddly held a flag. This was a man who was probably Evan but had red curly hair like Jamie's. I didn't really think anything of the drawing at the time, but now I wondered why she chose to draw what she did.

Looking around most of the drawings included the tall male stick figure had red curly hair, instead of dark or even yellow hair. Weird.

I continued my journey into picture history. I sorted through pictures of beautiful flowers I had come across, as well as, landmarks, historical sites, and breathtaking sunsets. The distinct edges of a Polaroid instant print picture stuck out from the middle of the remaining pictures. When I pulled it out, my stomach dropped. It was the picture Vince took the night the crew was in the bar. The entire crew was surrounding James and as he dipped me, kissing my lips with passion in this one. The sight of James took my breath away. I quickly shoved the photo into my purse and gathered up the rest of the pictures and put them into a shoebox to hide in my closet.

I needed to get going to be at the school in time for first day pick-up. I brushed my hair and put on a new coat of makeup. The bags under my eyes had disappeared and I almost looked like my normal self.

Evan walked in just as I grabbed my purse to leave.

"Where are you off to?" he asked.

"Jamie's getting outta school. I can't be late on her first day," I answered.

"Oh, that's right… but… okay, I guess you need to go. I just wanted us to have lunch together. I thought I'd surprise you." He lowered his head and spoke quietly.

"I can't right now. I've gotta run, maybe soon though?" I said, mostly as a question as I was hurrying out the door. I took a second to kiss him quickly.

I left him standing in the doorway.

CHAPTER 60

As fall moved into the area Evan and I grew even closer. We became more comfortable with each other, and my feelings began to grow.

I don't know why it was taking me so long to let my guard down. I'm not sure if it was the fact that I was so close to his sister, and that I used to know him when he ran around the house in Superman boxer shorts with red striped tube socks. I didn't think I was still holding on to the past. I gave up that pipe dream years before.

The night before Thanksgiving Evan and I were on a date that included a romantic dinner at a top-rated restaurant. I always looked for new dishes to try at my work. We weren't considered as ritzy as this place, but I might be able to get away with knockoff versions of some of their appetizers. We'd offer similar dishes for half the price. Knowing this it was hard to order anything off the menu without getting physically sick over the fact we were getting taken to the bank. It was hard to enjoy myself.

I had mentioned this many times, but Evan never cared. He still felt the need to wine and dine me to the nines. I would much rather order Chinese take-out or fix a good home cooked meal.

After eating my overpriced salmon with wild rice and drinking the wine that was aged twenty years for better flavor, not that it actually helped, I decided the least I could do was order the chocolate mousse. It was one of my favorite classy desserts.

I didn't notice Evan nervously fumbling in his pockets as I scooped large chocolate spoonfuls into my mouth. I choked when he got down one knee and opened a black velvet box. I knew immediately what was happening before I even noticed the two-carat solitaire glimmering back at me or heard Evan stumbling over the words he probably rehearsed for days before.

I looked around at the crowded restaurant and noticed everyone smiling and waiting in anticipation at my answer. I sat there open mouthed and looking confused but knowing with one hundred percent certainly what my answer was. I leaned in and hugged him and everyone around us assumed I said yes and turned toward their own dates forgetting the moment as quickly as it happened.

I whispered into his ear that we had to go. I was too embarrassed to stay here with everyone watching and would give him an answer as soon as we left.

He just looked into my eyes and held a solemn smile.

We got up and walked hand-in-hand out the door and once in the car I immediately explained why I couldn't answer him.

"I'm sorry for rushing out of there, Evan. That ring is… is… It's phenomenal. It's, it's just not for me. Not now. I'm not saying I don't ever want to accept it. I may. One day. But I just can't do it right now. It's too soon. We haven't even been dating a year yet." I stopped then and waited for him to respond.

"I'm sorry. I do understand. I love you. I thought this was the next step we'd need to take. It's okay, though. I'll just…keep this for another time," he sadly answered.

"Fair enough," I said, and hugged him tightly.

This may have been the first time he asked me to marry him, but it wouldn't be his last.

CHAPTER 61

One thing I noticed was that holidays were the time for Evan to bring the ring back out. I assumed he either thought substituting it for other presents was going to get him out of celebrating the holiday, or maybe he just thought they were spaced fairly even, and timing might be better.

Both were wrong.

On Christmas Eve we had just put Jamie down, and we were enjoying real eggnog by the lighted Christmas tree with holiday music from the radio. It was snowing outside, and big flakes could be seen falling by the street lights. It was a perfect Christmas Eve. That is, until Evan once again got down on his knee. This time I stopped him before he could even start talking. I simply shook my head slowly and he understood. I didn't need to explain, and he didn't want to argue. We sat silently beside each other for the next few hours.

We made love that night, but there was something missing. I knew I hurt his feelings, but I couldn't accept the ring if I truly didn't want to wear it. I knew in my heart I didn't want to marry him right now. I drifted off to sleep cradled in his arms. Whether I was half-awake or from somewhere in my dream I thought I heard Evan ask me why I kept saying no to him.

The next time he asked was fittingly on Valentine's Day. I knew it was coming. It was the holiday for lovers and probably the number one day for couples to get engaged. It had been rough recovering from Christmas when he tried to ask again so I prepared myself for the next time. I wrote out everything I loved about him and then wrote what I still needed us to do together before getting married.

I found myself making stuff up just to fill the second column. I had to. I just wasn't ready, again.

This time he asked over a quiet candlelit dinner at home. He showed up in a tuxedo. He said he had bought it for this day. I wish he would have saved his money.

When he got down on his knee again I simply smiled and prepared my speech. I let him talk, and then I started my pros and cons that I had planned.

"I love you, Evan. You need to know that. You are wonderful to me and Jamie. You take care of us and treat us like the world. Just please, I'm begging… give us some time," I said.

Then I continued with the cons. "But there is so much I still need to do and need you to do," I rattled off my long, and somewhat inventive list.

I even said I needed to pay off my student loans, not that I had any since James had paid my entire tuition. "I just don't want to join together with outstanding debt." I wondered if that sounded as corny to him as it did in my mind.

He took it well. Or, he pretended to at least. He kissed me and pocketed the ring patting it for good measure. "It'll remain right here, by my heart, until the next time."

I almost felt sorry for him. His holiday proposals were just too predictable.

CHAPTER 62

It was surprising when a Wednesday night during a non- holiday week in March brought the fourth and final proposal. This time I was caught off guard.

Evan didn't get down on one knee, nor did he pour his heart out with reasons on why we should get married. Instead he slid the ring across the kitchen bar and asked one question. "Is it the right time now?"

I'm not sure why he thought that was a good idea to do, especially with my hand dripping with raw chicken fat and the sink filled with scalding water to sanitize my skin to a red blistered mess to prevent E-coli. Being in the situation I was at that moment combined with his non-enthusiastic attitude put me over the edge of the "potential matrimony ledge."

I did the only thing I could. I laughed.

When he didn't say anything, I cleaned my hands and then elaborated on my feelings. "Evan, I really can't answer you right now. I'm sorry."

Not saying a word, he left the ring on the counter and turned and stormed out of the house, obviously upset.

When Jamie walked in and asked where Evan went I said he had to go somewhere, and I didn't know when he'd be back. Heck, I didn't know IF he would be back. I wasn't sad, mad, upset, or anything else. If anything I was relieved, given new room to breathe. I threw the ring into the silverware drawer and finished frying the chicken. Jamie and I ate together and had a great dinner.

That night when we watched cartoons and ate popcorn in pajamas and slippers we were the most relaxed we had been in a long time. We fell asleep on the couch with Sassy lying at our feet.

When I woke up and saw we were in the same spot I stroked Jamie's hair while the cat purred at my feet. I wondered why I ever thought I had to change this life.

CHAPTER 63

About a week after Evan walked out the door he was knocking on the same one. He immediately apologized, and I stopped him before he could finish.

"Listen, Evan, the time apart was exactly what I needed in order to make my decision. I now know that I don't want to marry you. I'm sorry it's not the answer you wanted me to give." I stopped him from coming inside.

I could tell he was upset. I never expected to hear what he said next. "What? Really? You're breaking up with me?"

Before I could tell him his leaving that night actually started the breakup he passed me and walked into the kitchen. Then he continued.

"You'll never be happy, Annie. You live in the past, and that Irish guy leaving hurt more than just you. My chance of having you was gone too when he left."

Now I was mad. "What exactly does that mean?"

He quickly answered, "It's like that time, when he called the bar sometime after he left, and I was in town. Mickey answered the phone when you were washing dishes."

I thought back but couldn't recall what time he was referring to.

"Well, Mickey mentioned it was that heroic red-headed beau of yours, probably calling to ride you off into the sunset. I grabbed the phone, told him you moved on, we were together, to not call again… I even think I said, 'If you wish to keep your legs or something'… I don't know. Mickey thought it was funny."

I was shocked, hurt, upset, stunned, and twenty-five other emotions boiling into one fiery explosion. I threw my glass against the door. It shattered into a pile of shards, and I told him he'd better follow in that same direction.

"I never, and I mean never want to see you again. I can't believe you wasted over a year of my life. But you know what? You're right. You're chances of ever having me are most certainly gone. But you are the only one that did that to yourself. Good-bye, Evan." I jammed my finger at the door and screamed for him to leave now.

Surprisingly, he did, without saying another word. I slid down into a stool and put my cheek down on the cool surface wondering where that "Annie" came from. I started laughing.

"I don't know, but I like her, and she'd better stay around," I said to myself.

CHAPTER 64

It didn't take me long to get over Evan. The worst part was explaining to Jamie that Evan wouldn't be coming around much anymore. Knowing there was potential for heartache for her was the one reason I never wanted to ever invite a man into my house.

By the following weekend I had completely de-Evaned my house. Every one of his toiletries and piece of his clothing was boxed up and sent back to his house through a mutual friend.

When he had started spending the nights at my house I even retired my pink and purple flowered quilt and bought a new man-friendly navy and white comforter. Before that weekend was over I had brought my favorite quilt back out from the closet and even added a few more throw pillows, which he hated.

I threw myself back into the pile of pillows and smiled at the ceiling. I knew that my lack of commitment and questionable feelings weren't me hanging on to the past. No matter what I pretended the reasoning was, it was actually the past hanging on to me.

I could never replace the love I had for James. And I knew I needed to begin my search again. Even if he rejected me completely he needed to know about his daughter. He needed to be part of her life and more importantly, she needed him in hers.

But the timing couldn't be worse.

Two weeks later, and before my true mission of finding James began, I received a phone call bearing bad news. A woman was on the other end of the phone asking for an Annie Blackwell and to see if she knew a Mr. Paul Blackwell.

"Yes," I answered. "I am Annie, and Mr. Blackwell is my...he is my father."

"Oh, good morning, ma'am. This is Dr. Dee Frazier. I am with Plains View Memorial Hospital here in Houston. You were listed on Mr. Blackwell's paperwork as next of kin. I'm so sorry to be the one to tell you, but your father passed away last night here at the hospital. He was brought in last evening by ambulance. We discovered it was an aneurism. I have a name here for you of the woman who came with him into the emergency room. It's Ms. Johnson, Lori Ann Johnson. I think she said she was his girlfriend. You may want to call her for more information. Again, I'm sorry for your loss."

I took down the number she recited and simply said 'Thank You' before hanging up.

The questions I now had were overwhelming. Did she just say my dad died? He had a girlfriend? He was indeed in Houston? He listed me as next of kin? Why would he do that? Had it really been this long since I thought or heard anything of him?

I immediately called Ms. Lori Ann Johnson, who had obviously been crying when she answered. After awkwardly introducing myself I asked her for the arrangement details and then told her I'd leave right away.

I had told Jamie we would plan a trip for her fifth birthday. I didn't think it would be to her unknown grandfather's funeral.

I had so much to do that I didn't have time to think. I immediately jumped up from the bed and grabbed two suitcases. I didn't know how long we would be gone, so I went through a mental checklist of what Jamie and I would need and threw everything into the cases. My idea was to do that first, and then make a checklist of things missed as I did the rest of the tasks needed before leaving.

I found Jamie looking at books on her bedroom floor and told her I was surprising her with a trip. "Mommy has something we need to do in Texas. Do you know where that is, honey?"

"Is it in Pennsylvanney?" she asked.

"No, it's far away and will take us a while to get there. We have a lot to do before we leave." I opened her dresser drawers for clothes to pack.

"OK. Can I help you do what needs to be done?"

I hugged her. "You sure can."

As Jamie was distracted with finding a few small toys to take I called Laura to tell her the news. She was now in Florida and worked as a flight attendant, so she could easily fly and get tickets in an emergency such as this.

She said she'd find us tickets and then meet us there as soon as she could.

"Sit tight, sis. I'll call you as soon as I have news on the flights. I love you," she added.

"Ok, we'll be ready. I love you, too." I knew the tickets would be standby and could be available as soon as an hour, or as late as a day from now.

I then made three phone calls. The first was to my boss, Frank, to let him know I wouldn't be in for a while. Frank, as a boss, was second only to Joey, he was caring and understanding and even though I hadn't missed much work I still felt sorry to ask him to cover my shifts. Then, I called Jamie's school. I left a message explaining the situation and gave my number to call to confirm the message. Last, I called Gram and Pap. I gave them the news.

"Honey, I'm so sorry. Even though he hasn't been around I still know he's still your only father," Gram told me.

"I'll call when we get there," I said.

"Be safe. Give Laura and Jamie a kiss from us." Then she said goodbye.

CHAPTER 65

After filling our suitcases to the point of sitting on them for better closure I made arrangements for a neighbor to watch Sassy. Just as I finished pre-making sandwiches for the plane and adding water bottles to two carry-on bags my phone rang.

"Your flight leaves at 2:50, you'll have a layover in Chicago and will arrive in Houston at 7:30. I'll be leaving at 4:20 and should get in by nine o'clock," she quickly explained. I wrote down the details. "And when I get there I'll find us a hotel. I'll call you and let you know where we're staying.

Ten minutes later I was locking the front door. Jamie had Birdie gripped in both hands as we climbed into the cab. She immediately began a barrage of questions. *When will we get there? How long will it take? What will we do when we get there?*

Occupying my time with answering her twenty questions kept me from thinking about the circumstances. We were still about a mile from the airport when she finally ran out of things to ask, and I actually began to think of what happened today.

The father I'd never known came back into my life, but only as a name with the words "passed away" following it. I knew I should be crying, but I'd be cheating myself since I had no reason to be able to conjure up such an emotion.

A large jet flew over and caught Jamie's eye. "Holy Smokey, look at that!" She gasped with excitement. "Are we going to be on that plane?"

The airline emblem on the tail was the same one we'd be flying on. "It just might be. Are you excited about your first plane ride?"

She instantly looked nervous. "A little…I guess. I'm a lot afraid of heights and don't know if I want to look out the window."

"It's okay, you don't have to if you don't want to, but I bet you'll change your mind when we get up in the sky." I stroked her hand.

When we pulled up to the curb I paid the driver, and he quickly brought the bags around to the side of the car for us. Laura had said to go to the VIP counter for the tickets. I didn't feel like I deserved a VIP status, and was embarrassed as all eyes of the long line of customers waiting to check in followed us to the vacant lane where I was instructed to go.

The airline attendant's tag read "Glenda", and she seemed glad to see us. After tagging our luggage and the carry-on bags we would be taking with us she pinned a set of plastic wings on Jamie's shirt for her first flight. Then she shook her small hand and handed her a certificate signed by a pilot welcoming her aboard the 737 that she will be riding in today.

Watching her eyes light up with excitement brought tears to my own. She looked up at me as we turned to leave and cupping her hand over her small mouth whispered, "Okay, I think I might just wanna look out the window now."

CHAPTER 66

We were early for our flight, but I certainly didn't need to find things to occupy Jamie. She stood with her forehead pressed to the glass window watching the planes take off and land. She laughed as the luggage carts zoomed around and the men guiding planes with their "orange flashlights" as she called them.

I tried to get her to sit down and eat something since we didn't even have lunch, but she didn't want to miss anything. I don't blame her. The first flight is always the most exciting adventure. I remembered mine very well.

Gram and Pap decided to take my sister and me to Disney World the year after mom passed away. To cheer us up, Gram planned every detail of the trip including down to where we would eat and what we would see each day. I remember a red guidebook and highlighter that Gram carried with her everywhere, and she would make notes frequently throughout the days before our trip.

Laura and I were so excited we packed a week in advance and had to live in old clothes and without our favorite toys, since everything we loved was ready to go to Florida. The night before we left, we slept together on the couch, in full dress including shoes. We didn't want to miss the trip and certainly wouldn't be able to since the couch was beside the front door.

I remember when we arrived at the airport. I felt like a million dollars. In my eyes I was rich since I was able to travel like the business people I saw hurrying toward their gates. It was amazing, comparable to an amusement park. People running, voices talking over the loud speaker, lights, televisions, and gates in every direction. I followed close to Gram and Pap and didn't want to get too far from their sight in fear of being washed away in the crowd of travelers.

When we made it to our gate we still had an hour to spare before being able to board. My sister and I were in awe watching the big planes out the window. We pretended to be on each one that went by and made up a new flight plan with each take off. She was going to China. I went to France. We both liked the idea of the beach, no matter where it was so she chose Mexico, and I went to Hawaii. Pap pulled us from our trips around the world when they called us to finally board.

Take off was fun for us. The way we were pressed back into our seats felt like a roller coaster taking off. Gram said she liked the landing more, because it meant we made it back to earth.

When we got to Orlando they had been having torrential downpours all week, and it didn't let up during the 5 days we were there. We barely got through a third of what she planned in her guidebook, and the one thing my sister and I couldn't talk enough about was the plane rides to and from Orlando. My Pap wouldn't let Gram live that trip down for a long time.

A flashback took me back to that moment by the window when I laid my head on the cold glass and watched the planes taxi in and take off. Laura and I hadn't moved during the entire hour. Now, years later I could feel the coldness of the glass again through my child. I would let her enjoy these moments because just like Orlando, I didn't know what Houston would bring.

Lunch could wait.

CHAPTER 67

The first plane ride held the same amusement park feeling for Jamie that it did for me when I was younger. As we were boarding the second flight out of Chicago, she was ready for the trip to be over.

"Mommy, I like taking trips, but I'm ready to get there already," she said.

"Soon, sweetheart. Traveling takes time, but we'll be there before you know it," I answered.

I knew she was tired so I held her close in our seats in the middle of the plane and stroked her hair, running my fingers slowly through her ringlet curls.

Within minutes of take-off, I could hear her soft but deep breathing. I paged through an airline-supplied magazine with my free hand and waved off the flight attendant as she sweetly asked if we wanted drinks. I didn't want Jamie to wake up, even sacrificed my arm to the pins and needles of falling asleep in order to not disturb her by moving it.

She slept the entire way. As we touched down she was jerked awake and sleepily looked around as if wondering where she was and how she got there.

"Mornin' sunshine." I joked.

"We're here? Already?" She asked.

"Yes, and you took a very long nap." I shook my hand to wake it up.

I checked my watch – eight thirty Eastern Time which was seven thirty in Houston. We were right on time.

I held Jamie's hand as we gathered our bags. Then, making our way to the information booth I asked where the best hotels would be. We needed to find a room before we did anything else.

The older woman, whose name badge read Constance, told me about one that was two miles down the road. She gave me the number and even let me use her desk phone, so I didn't have to dig my cell phone out of my bottomless purse.

Ten minutes later we were booked at the Houston Inn and Suites and headed for an awaiting taxi. Jamie silently followed every move I made.

She stared out the window from the backseat of the cab. It was getting dark, and this was actually her bed time back home. I was thankful she took the long nap that she did.

"Mommy, I'm really hungry," she said.

"I am, too. That's the first thing we'll do when we get there," I told her.

I paid the cab driver when he pulled up to the drive of the hotel and scanned the area for restaurants. There was a sub shop, fast food burger joint, and a pizza place.

"Let me get the room taken care of and we'll order pizza," I said, paying the cab driver.

A young man, who looked to still be in his teens checked us into our room and even ordered a medium cheese pizza to be delivered.

"They're so fast I'll probably be calling before you get into your room." He laughed.

"I hope so. We're starving," I told the teenager.

He was almost right. I had thrown the suitcases on the bed and turned the television on to a cartoon for Jamie when the phone rang.

We ate the best cheese pizza ever created by man, and I was unpacking when I heard Jamie ask me to read something she noticed out the window.

"What's that say, Mommy?" She pointed.

I read out loud.

"*Erin Go Bragh.* I think it means, *Ireland forever.* It looks like a restaurant. Maybe we can eat there tomorrow."

CHAPTER 68

Around nine thirty Laura was knocking on the door. She had gotten my message on where we were staying, and like our plane, hers was on time as well.

I hugged her, and after dropping her luggage on the other bed she leaned over and kissed Jamie on her forehead as she slept with the television glow reflecting on her face.

"It was a long day for her," I explained.

"For us too," she said turning her attention back to me opening her arms for another hug.

"Yeah, I'm sorry we had to get together under these circumstances."

"It feels weird. We didn't even know the guy. I almost feel guilty for being here," she said.

"But he's our dad. Besides, Lori Ann Johnson there is nobody else that he had in his life. We have to be there." She opened her suitcase and began to unload the contents.

I left her to unpack and took a trip down the hall to the ice machine. I just needed a few minutes to collect my thoughts. So much has happened to me in the last few days. Everything was so overwhelming. Now, with the funeral I just didn't know how much deeper this hole could get before it caved in, and I wouldn't be able to climb back out.

I needed to ground myself before I jumped off the earth. I bought the biggest chocolate bar I could find in the vending machine and fell back into a lounge chair by the bank of windows that overlooked the city. I wished I had my mom here to confide in, for my sister and me to hug once again. It was crazy to think that I wasn't even thirty years old, and both my parents were now gone.

I let the memories race around my mind as I tore open the wrapper to my chocolate bar and dove in. I never was a comfort-eater, but today seemed to be the exception.

That morning I had woken up happy. Now, just twelve hours later I was a whirlwind of emotion, dipped in rich dark chocolate.

I felt like crying, but knew that it wouldn't help and would just feel forced. I lost my dad and took my daughter out of school only to keep secret the real reason for our mini-vacation. I am seeing my sister for the first time in almost three years, and here I sit, on a chair, in a hotel I never imagined I'd be in.

The sound of ice falling in the machine to my right startled me. I was then aware of the smell of chlorine-infused sheets and carpet cleaner. I was halfway through my sweet treat when I noticed something blink out of the corner of my eye. It was the sign for the Erin Go Bragh restaurant.

As if in synchronization the "I" in the sign fizzled and blinked followed by the "go." *I go… That's odd. I go… I go where?* I wondered as I headed back to the room.

CHAPTER 69

Laura and I were sitting beside each other at a window table in Mama's Café, a small restaurant that we were told had the best breakfast in Texas. We watched every car that pulled up and every person that walked past. We were meeting Lori Ann.

As we waited I began to tell Jamie the real reason for our visit. I showed her a picture of her grandfather from years before. I didn't know if he had even looked the same, but I wanted her to get an idea of who he was.

"Honey, your grandfather passed away," I explained.

She looked at me like my head was glowing and my ears were shooting purple flames.

"He went to be with Jesus," I continued.

She understood. "So we won't get to visit him?"

I shook my head and then gave her a hug.

Laura looked over with compassion in her eyes, and as we sat there in silence we were interrupted by a middle-aged woman with perfectly fixed blonde hair and wafting in on the smell of a hair salon.

"Ya'll must be Paul's girls," she said, holding her hand out before reaching the table.

I could tell she was as nervous as I was. "Yes, I'm Annie." I shook her offered hand.

I introduced Jamie and Laura and told her how sorry we were for her loss. She briefly looked down and bit her lip before sliding into the vacant chair across from me. I could see how fresh the wound was for her.

After a couple of extra-long minutes, she looked across the table at us.

171

"You have a lot of questions, I'm sure," she said, slightly above a whisper.

I nodded and could see Laura doing the same out of the corner of my eye.

Then she quickly began telling her story. "Well, let me first tell you that I loved your dad more than anything in the world. We were together for two glorious years, but have known each other since the day he moved here. I was the desk clerk at the hotel he checked into that first night. I was married then, and it wasn't until three or four years ago we happened to be standing in the same line at JJ's Quick Stop that we started a conversation and became truly good friends.

"He was trying to win me over, and I was just getting out of a bad divorce. I ignored him for months." She quietly chuckled, thinking back to that time.

And then she continued. "I finally gave in, and not long after that we became a couple. He told me about you girls. He said he truly missed you and wished it could have been different. He wanted to know where you were and what happened, but time wasn't on his side, and he never got the chance."

Laura stopped her. "You don't have to defend him or explain anything. We grew up fine and are still fine today."

Lori Ann looked deflated.

It was my turn. "We're sorry. Neither one of us means to hurt you, and we don't want to badmouth a man that isn't even here to defend himself. He knew where we were. He could have visited anytime, or at least called. He didn't even know about his granddaughter."

I pulled Jamie close to me and continued. "I'm here because I chose to be. After all these years I still respect my father enough to do that for him."

"I agree," Laura said beside me.

"Fair enough," Lori Ann replied. "The arrangements are made for the funeral tomorrow afternoon, with a viewing in the morning. He didn't want anything big, that much I know."

She gave us directions to the funeral home, and we said we'd be there. Then, as she walked away she turned and looked over her shoulder. "It was nice to finally meet you. I'm sorry it had to be under these circumstances."

"You too, Lori Ann. Thank you for everything, and…and for being there with our father," I said to her.

She simply smiled and nodded.

Laura and I sat and stared at each other for a few minutes. It was an awkward moment, but I don't think either one of us could think of anything to say.

Jamie broke the silence. "That lady was very nice. She seemed sad, but she was really nice. Can I have some scrambled eggs now?"

I laughed. "Of course you can."

CHAPTER 70

As much as we all wanted to explore Houston we weren't here on vacation and couldn't relax until after the funeral. I had left our house in such a hurry that I hadn't packed Jamie or myself proper clothes for a funeral. All three of us spent the next five and a half hours trying on dresses and shoes from thirteen different stores.

When we finally found outfits that worked Jamie passed out in the backseat with her head resting on the window, and I rubbed my feet while sitting in the passenger side.

"I had so much fun shopping with you girls today," Laura replied, pulling into our hotel in her rented sedan.

I looked at her with raised eyebrows." Are you crazy?"

"No, why?" She laughed.

"This… what we did today… this is the reason I hate shopping. I didn't have any fun and just want to soak my tired feet in the tub, along with the rest of my body," I said, realizing once again how opposite my sister and I really were.

"Well, I'm going to drop you off so you can take a bath, and Jamie can finish her nap, and I'm going to find us some dinner." She pulled up to the door.

"Sounds good. In fact, it sounds perfect. If you grab the bags I'll carry Jamie to the room."

Five minutes later I had the water running in the tub and was pulling the curtains closed to keep Jamie from waking. I stopped and stared at the restaurant below. Cars were starting to fill the parking lot, and I realized I had told Jamie we'd go there for dinner. We still had a few days before we had to go home. I would make a point to take her there soon.

With the tub overflowing with bubbles from the trial size shampoo bottle offered from housekeeping I sank low into the water and closed my eyes, feeling myself relax for the first time since hearing the news of my father's death.

It only seemed like a few seconds before I heard the card reader of the door letting me know Laura had made it back with dinner. I opened my eyes and took one last deep breath before having to get out of the tub.

Quickly drying off I pulled my satin robe around me and tied the belt tightly.

"You're back sooner than I thought you'd be," I whispered, but noticed Jamie open her eyes and smile at me from the far bed. "And whatever you have smells so good."

"It's barbecue from right over there," she nodded out the window.

"Erin Go Bragh's? Really? I wanted to try that place and actually told Jamie we'd go there," I said excitedly. "But barbecue? At an Irish restaurant?

"I know, right? Their menu looked fantastic, but this was the special." She started to remove the to-go containers from the paper bag.

The ribs and brisket were to die for. The meat was tender, fell off the bone, and was dripping with sauce. It was the best food my lips had ever tasted. I ate until my stomach hurt. Even Jamie, the picky eater that I unfortunately was raising ate everything on her plate and asked for seconds, which I gladly dished out to her.

"I know where we're going after the funeral tomorrow. I can't wait to see what else they have to offer." I laid back on the bed and closed my eyes.

"It's been a long day. Let's watch a couple movies," Laura suggested.

Jamie jumped up and down beside me on the bed and screamed about a new princess movie that she saw advertised.

We couldn't say no to that excitement, so that is just what we spent the evening watching.

CHAPTER 71

The next day we were eerily quiet as we got ready to go to the funeral home. Even Jamie, who was usually bouncing off the walls in the morning, had finished putting on her shoes and was now lying completely still against a huge pile of pillows on the bed. Her eyes, non-blinking, stayed fixed on the cartoons on television.

"I can't take this silence. It's like someone died around here." Laura laughed, hoping to lighten the mood.

I spit coffee across the table. "Laura!"

"Hey, I don't want to be here anymore than you do. I just want to get there, get this over with, and go back to the life I had two days ago," she quickly explained. "Might as well lighten things up and go into this with at least a smile."

"True. But the reason I'm so quiet is because I really don't know how to feel. Shouldn't I be crying by now?" I asked.

"You know, that is exactly how I feel," she agreed. "I thought something must be wrong with me."

As I tried to conjure up tears, or even sadness, I realized it just wasn't going to happen. It seemed like the emotion that should come with a funeral, like it did with our mom's, was void this time.

One thing we both knew was we weren't ready to face Lori Ann again. It was awkward yesterday and would be even harder to do knowing the one person we had in common now laid in a coffin between us. Because of this, we didn't want to get to the funeral home too early. While we waited for the morning to pass I told her about my break-up with Evan.

"I knew he wasn't your type! He's too goody-goody, uppity, and just… just… too clean cut," she said, with no surprise in her voice.

"Yes, he was a pretty boy. He even took longer showers than me and Jamie combined. I just don't think I ever was really in love with him. Again, I should have felt more emotion when we broke up. Maybe I just don't have any feelings anymore," I said, more to myself than as part of the conversation.

Laura was holding a large clip in her mouth as she twisted her hair into a loose bun. "Row rhat?" she asked through clenched lips.

"No, what?" I asked, thinking how much she sounded like a cartoon dog at that moment.

She paused, finishing her beauty regime before speaking again. "I just remembered something I was going to tell you last night. You know how I got take-out from that place over there?" She nodded her head out the window.

"Yes."

"Well there is this really cute guy that works there. And when I saw him I totally thought he was your type. Maybe dumping Evan before coming here was the best thing you could have done," she said.

I shook my head. "No way sis, don't even think about it! You are the worst matchmaker known to man! Remember Robbie, ninth grade?"

She scrunched her forehead remembering back to that time. "Oh.... Yeah, that didn't work well, did it? But I swear I didn't know he liked piercings that much."

We both laughed together, and I glanced at the clock. It was time to finally leave.

"Well, how about we go eat there this evening and you can check out the scenery for yourself?" She winked.

I just smiled and shook my head again. I didn't know what to say. I just wanted the funeral to be over. I would have probably agreed to anything Laura suggested as long as it meant this day was on the fast track to being over.

CHAPTER 72

The directions to the funeral home took us to a very small town west of Houston. The two-lane road we followed ended at a stop sign fronting a bank and town hall in what looked like an old converted mill. There was a diner that was closed, and two oddly placed antique stores. The funeral home was two streets down from the bank and was roughly the size of a mid-size sedan.

"Wow. This should be interesting," I whispered.

Laura could only agree. Jamie, on the other hand, was fascinated at the sight of cows crowding a fence by the road. "Look, Mommy, cows in town!"

Pulling into the parking lot of Smith and Dodd Funeral Home we could see only a handful of other cars. "Are we early or late?" Laura asked.

I looked at the clock in the car, "Neither. People around here must just carpool."

Mr. Dodd, the funeral director, greeted us at the door. "Laura and Annie. So good to meet you. I'm sorry it's under these circumstances," he said in his best sympathetic tone.

I nodded, but thought how odd what he was saying sounded. Good to meet us? Under these circumstances? In what other life would he ever meet us anyway?

His lingering handshake bothered me, especially when he patted my forearm with his other cold hand. I was actually very relieved to see Lori Ann approach us.

She hugged all three of us without saying anything and then led us down the hall to the lone viewing room. There were three rows of chairs in a room that couldn't hold more than twenty people. At the far wall the casket sat with a long spray of red and white roses across the top.

I felt nauseous from the smell and was glad to see the casket was closed. A display of photographs sat on an easel to the side of the casket and Jamie, who had been holding tightly on to my arm, quickly ran to look at the pictures. Not wanting to have to look at my dad's casket I followed. Laura was right behind me.

Besides Lori Ann, there were only four other people in the room, and all eyes were on us. Whispers gave away that each person was talking about us. I didn't know any of them and didn't care to meet them, now, or ever. I decided then that I would stay by that easel, memorizing each photo if I had to as long as I didn't have to talk about the dad I couldn't remembered.

CHAPTER 73

After an excruciating two hours Mr. Dodd ushered our small group into another room that resembled a chapel. "It's time to start the service," he said in a soft voice, just barely audible.

I sighed and pulled Jamie close to me after selecting the first pew we came to. She had been very well behaved during the entire visitation, mostly because she made friends with the resident Persian cat.

Mr. Dodd had explained that Nancy, which was indeed the cat's name, was once a kitten of an unlikely customer who visited the funeral home; unlucky because the lady who was the owner was in a casket herself. The cat wouldn't leave. It was just too creepy for me to understand. Just another reason I couldn't wait to get out of there.

I guess I shouldn't have been surprised when Mr. Dodd asked my sister and I if we wanted to say a few words. Laura sat in a puddle of tears. She had warned me that funerals make her cry, no matter who it was for; so much for her not being able to cry. She didn't tell me though that she would be a blubbering idiot. I stood up and walked to the podium where Mr. Dodd stood with his fingers intertwined in front of him. His eyes held the sympathy he didn't need to say aloud.

I looked out at the people in front of me. Lori Ann smiled and slightly nodded her head. Laura had one arm around Jamie and the other hand shoved a tissue over her nose. Besides those three, there were only six more people in the room. Mr. Dodd stood to my left. Two women in their seventies sat in the pew behind Laura. A couple, presumably Lori Ann's daughter and son-in-law sat with her. Finally, there was a gentleman with graying hair and glasses in the law pew at the back.

Ten people in all.

Only ten people were at my father's funeral. How sad is that? Nobody should only have ten people at their funeral. I closed my eyes to keep the hot tears from spilling out and quickly said what I felt most. "I wish I could have had more father-daughter time. I wish he could have known my daughter, or even knew that he had a grandchild. I wish it could have been different… for all of us."

When I got back to the pew I felt a single tear splash on my hand. I stared at it like it was a foreign germ invading my body. I guess I really did still have feelings.

CHAPTER 74

With my arm around Jamie's small shoulders, I robotically stroked her arm in a circular pattern. I watched the rest of the service in a distorted cloud, afraid to blink for fear that the tears would streak my make-up.

I would have worn waterproof mascara had I thought I would actually cry.

As Mr. Dodd thanked the nine of us for coming I stood slowly and Laura hugged both of us, sandwiching Jamie in the middle.

"I love you, sis. The hard part is over now," she whispered into my hair.

My only response was a nod.

I felt a tap on my shoulder and slowly turned to see the gentleman who had been sitting at the back as the one that poked me.

"You're Annie, right?" he asked.

"Yes," I wiped my cheek quickly.

He held out his hand but instead of offering to shake mine he held out a tissue.

I thanked him and blotted quickly under my eyes noting that there was no way any mascara survived.

"My name is Steve Copeland," he quickly offered.

When we didn't show recognition at his name he continued, "I was your dad's next-door neighbor... more importantly, his attorney."

"Oh, nice to meet you Steve." I shook his hand and introduced Laura and Jamie.

"I had to catch you before you leave because if not mistaken both of you flew in for the funeral, correct?" he asked.

"Yes, that's correct," I asked with curiosity growing as to where this conversation was going.

"Can I ask how long you're in for?" he asked while reaching into his back pocket.

"Actually, since we're done with what we came for we were just going to see about heading out tomorrow. Both of us have to get back to work," Laura answered before I could say anything.

"Oh. I see." He looked defeated, but I could practically see the wheels turning in his head.

Instead of asking the obvious question of why he needed to know, I waited, knowing my answer would come within the next few seconds.

"I really need for you to come by my office... bad thing is I'm in court the next two days. I'm not free until Friday," he indeed answered my question.

"Can I ask why, Steve?" I was anxious to leave and by now there was nobody but Lori Ann left in the room and she appeared to be finalizing things with Mr. Dodd.

"Why for the will, of course," he said.

I looked at Laura and saw the same surprise and confusion in her face that I had.

Now, two more questions lingered. Why didn't I know there was a will? More importantly, why were we even in it?

CHAPTER 75

We set the appointment for the first available time he had available. It would be at nine o'clock am Friday morning. This meant that we would have to stay in Houston for another three days.

I called my Gram and Pap, Jamie's school, and work, in that order. I didn't bother with Evan or anyone else. I was beginning to realize my ties to Pennsylvania were getting thinner than ever. Knowing this, I didn't mind staying away for the rest of the week. And with the funeral now behind us we could actually begin to have somewhat of a vacation.

"I know, it's morbid to think that I'm using this trip as a vacation but with running the restaurant I really don't have time to take a true getaway vacation," I explained to Laura. "I've been promising to do something with Jamie for months now, but something always comes up at the restaurant that makes our plans change."

"I understand. Since we've moved back to the states and I bravely decided to take the job with the airline I've been busier than I could ever imagine. I always thought flight attendants saw the world. I've only seen airports around the world and national monuments from thousands of feet in the air while strapped into my landing seat. How about we ask the desk clerk for a "must do" list for this fine city and let's hit it all," she suggested.

Ten minutes later, after arriving back at the hotel we did just that. The woman at the counter gladly gave us a list of top ten tourist attractions in the Houston area, a fistful of brochures for local sites, and suggestions for her favorite places to see and eat. It was overwhelming.

The clerk had just told us where to find the best desserts and coffee but apparently didn't get the chance to talk about what she, herself, enjoyed doing in the area so she offered an earful to us. "And now don't go to the Shipman's down on 5th Street. They don't clean the bathrooms as well as the other two in the city. But the one on Anderson... oh, they keep their food under the heat lamp too long. I guess that leaves the one on the other side of the city but you probably don't want to go that far to find something to eat. There are also a few good Chinese restaurants, ohhh, or Mexican. Houston has some great Mexican restaurants. If you get the chance, try Dos Hombres. They always win awards for their food."

I stared at the woman wide-eyed while Laura nodded acting as she was taking in everything she had to say. My stomach heard her talking about all the food and made me cut her speech short. "Wow, so much to do. I can't wait to get started."

I knew Houston was big but the hotel was located outside the city and there was really nothing around for miles to do. Nothing, that is but an out of place Irish named restaurant oddly placed beside this even more out of place hotel.

"Mommy, I'm hungry," Jamie whispered up to me as if reading what my mind was just thinking.

"Me too. It's been a long day," I said. "Let's go change out of these sad clothes and see what else this restaurant over here has to offer. If it's anything like we had last night we may not want to ever leave this city."

CHAPTER 76

"What a jerk!" I yelled, aiming my anger to the driver of the blue pickup truck who just pulled out in front of us.

"Calm down, sister! I should be the one mad. I'm the one driving," Laura said after slamming on the brakes.

"Well we only had to drive two blocks and lucky us to have the pleasure to come across that dumb..." I caught myself before saying what I really wanted to say. "And why did we drive again?"

Laura laughed. "It's a thousand degrees outside. I know you aren't used to hot weather but being that I'm made of pure sugar I just might melt in this heat."

It was my turn to laugh. Jamie joined in and innocently as ever asked, "Well, Mommy if Aunt Laura is sugar, what are you made of then?"

"Vinegar," Laura answered without missing a beat.

"Ha! Yeah right. Get out of the car, both of you. We're here."

The wonderful smells of smoked meat and fried foods met us at the entrance to the restaurant. Incredibly my stomach instantly grew hungrier than I was before and I couldn't wait to order everything on the menu even without knowing what was on there.

I held the door open for Jamie and Laura and smiled at the hostess who stood inside waiting to seat us.

"Hey ya'll. Welcome to Erin Go Bragh's. Three today?"

"Yes, ma'am," I said, realizing how odd the southern accent sounded with the Irish name of the restaurant.

I followed in behind our party train and could just hear the waitress make small talk with Laura in the front. As we walked, I took in the décor and atmosphere of the restaurant. It was amazing to say the least.

The wood throughout was stained dark mahogany and the table-tops were each painted with Irish countryside scenes and covered with a thick pane of glass to protect the finish. I was stunned at how beautiful the craftsmanship was. It was a far cry from the bar-like look of the outside.

The hostess listed the specials of the day and offered a recommendation of the "sweeten-it-yourself" southern- style sweet tea. She then let us know the waitress would be by shortly.

I thanked her while searching the menu for the children's section. Before I could name off what they had Jamie was shouting for a cheeseburger and fries. That was easy.

It didn't take me long to decide either. As soon as my eyes saw the it, I knew I would have the authentic Texas Brisket sandwich with Sweet Potato Fries, creamy cole slaw and of course the recommended sweet tea. It seemed like the perfect southern meal for the day we had.

Dawn, our waitress, sashayed up to our table with a covered basket and small bowl on her tray. "Hi guys. Do you know what you want to drink? Or even order?" She saw our folded menus on the table.

We quickly ordered and before Dawn left she set the two mystery items down in the middle of us. Laura and I looked at each other and she slowly peeled the corner back. I expected rolls. Surprisingly it was a basket of homemade chips and the bowl held barbeque sauce. We each took one and tasted the sweet mesquite sauce. What a great combination. The way this tasted though I knew I'd need to stop myself or I wouldn't be able to eat my meal.

As I dipped and ate the crispy chips I found myself scanning the restaurant in hopes of finding the mysterious guy Laura talked about the night before. For some reason I felt the need to see him but there were only women working that night.

"Now remember, we have a lot of food coming," I told Jamie, warning her, and myself that too much of a good thing isn't always good for you.

CHAPTER 77

If I could have found a volunteer to carry me out of the restaurant I would have done just that. I was so full and from the moans from the other two in my party I believe they were too.

"Fantastic," was the simple word to describe the food.

"Yes, it was." I agreed with Laura.

When we got back to the hotel it was just getting dark and we stopped at the front desk to let them know about your needed extension on our room. The parking lot had been empty the entire time we were there so I didn't think they'd have a problem accommodating us.

I wonder how a place could stay in business that was this far from town. The hotel seemed so out of place. It was extremely gorgeous and extravagantly large but it was just dropped in the middle of nowhere. I couldn't help it, I had to find out why.

The overly friendly lady at the front desk was quick to respond, "It's to introduce growth toward the suburban areas... the city is just so crowded that the governor, mayor, or someone in the political arena thought it would be a good idea to start out here and move backward toward the city. I'm just hoping they catch up soon before we have to close from not having enough business."

I thanked her for the clarification and excused our group before being trapped any further in conversation. I skipped a shower and changed into pajamas. Laura and Jamie did the same and after only watching a few minutes of a movie we all fell asleep.

As soon as I drifted off I began to dream. It had been months since I had a "James-mare" and I was afraid for what I would experience. Usually I would end up crying throughout the entire night and waking up miserable, extremely sad, and upset with not making myself stop mid-dream.

This time, I could tell right away it was different. I was with James and we were riding in a convertible. I was hugging on his arm and he was whistling into my ear making me squirm from being tickled with his beard. I could just make out the song, it was Annie's Song, the one he played at the bar. That made me smile and hold onto him even more.

When I looked out the front window again it had turned dark and the air was now chilly. I wrapped up in the blanket I had somehow been holding. It smelled just like the soap he used. I lifted my eyes to look into his as I buried my nose into the soft fabric. I realized then it was one of his flannel shirts he'd wear around after work.

Then, I asked him where we were going. I knew we were in the car for a long time. I didn't want the trip to end but my curiosity peaked as bright lights of a city came into view.

"Houston, my love," he said between notes he was whistling.

"Good. I need you to meet someone," I said.

Then, as if on cue, Jamie called out for me. I woke up to see the clock read 4:51 am.

What a wonderful dream.

CHAPTER 78

"Mommy, I don't feel good," Jamie said, rubbing her stomach. I felt her head. She was warm.

Counting back the days as my mom taught me I realized three days ago would have put us on the plane. The flu or other illnesses would have been flying rampant around the airport and within the unclean ventilation system.

Perfect. Just what we needed.

I helped her to the bathroom and just as she knelt on the tile her half-digested dinner resurfaced in the toilet.

I could hear her apologize but I silenced her by petting her head and holding her hair as a momma's job description describes. A wet washcloth at hand and trash can propped by the side of the bed we were ready to go back to sleep by ten after five. I held her by my side as Laura silently slept in the other bed, completely unaware of what just occurred.

At six thirty-two startling sounds awoke me: the sound of Jamie getting ready to be sick again, and the pounding rain on the glass.

Rain and the Flu. What next?

Before I could get up to help Jamie I heard a moan from the other bed. "Annie," Laura whispered.

"Yes," I walked toward her.

"I really don't feel well. I'm achy... so achy. Every single thing on my body hurts. And my head is killing me," she moaned again.

Ok, rain and dual flu patients. Now it's perfect, I thought sarcastically.

CHAPTER 79

After getting seventeen minutes worth of directions to a drug store from Connie—the woman from the front desk—I headed out to get medicine for the two sick patients.

When I got back to the hotel I emptied the bags onto the table. I had grabbed everything I could find that might help— including ginger ale, Lysol, and saltine crackers--staples for the flu.

I remembered that I also brought my anti-nausea medicine with me on the trip. Pouring two glasses of ginger ale and forcing a couple crackers into each patient's mouth I followed both up with the anti-nausea medicine. I knew they would be asleep the rest of the day after that took effect.

So I sat in the chair at the table and watched the silent screen of the television. Eventually, I knew that both had fallen asleep. Unlike them I knew I needed to get something to eat. I was starving.

"I'll just run next door and grab something quick," I told myself as I glanced in the mirror and ran my fingers through my now flat hair. Deciding the only hope for it was up, I gathered all my hair and twirled it around holding it in place and finally jabbing a pen through the loose bun. That felt so much better.

My purse was sitting on the bathroom sink and as I walked I pulled makeup out of it and applied it blindly down the hallway. I used the reflective elevator door to check my work. I wanted to make sure I would get back before they woke up, even though I knew that wouldn't happen with all the medicines they were on.

Still I rushed. I rarely got time to myself. I was always racing to get back to Jamie. With her being sick I felt bad leaving just to get something to eat.

I slid into the barstool at Erin Go Braugh's. I knew this would the fast way to get my food. A woman pouring a beer from a tap smiled at me to let me know I was there. I smiled back. Then, as if she saw a ghost she looked again and held my gaze as her eyes grew large. She was shaken back to reality when the beer she was pouring ran over the glass and splashed onto her shoes.

I furrowed my eyebrows and lightly shook my head wondering what I was missing. She wiped her hands, apologizing as she came over to me. She continued to stare, which was disturbing, yet somewhat flattering, like I was a movie star but didn't know it yet.

"Hello, I'm Josie," she said. "Can I get you a drink?"

Before I could remember that I needed to be in a hurry I ordered a rum and cola. I almost told her to stop making it and to hurry with a menu for my food order but my mind told me to stop and enjoy a moment. I took a deep breath as if to punctuate that thought.

I drank in silence as I waited for my food order. I was well aware of people looking at me but I focused on my glass and twirled my stirring straw between my fingers. I barely swallowed the last swig before Josie was in front of me asking if I wanted another one. I nodded and saw my to-go bag of food get set on the bar.

"You look so familiar," Josie said after setting the bag down in front of me. "How do I know you?"

"We're staying over at the hotel across the street. We've eaten here before," I offered explanation while trying to down the second drink I'd just been delivered.

She nodded but did so with doubt. There was more to it than just being a past customer.

I could see it too but hurried to finish the drink in order to leave as quickly as possible. The way that everyone was looking at me made me very uncomfortable.

The kitchen door swung open and another woman, older than Josie, came out carrying a clipboard and was visibly upset. She slammed the clipboard down on the bar and pointed at something on the paper. "The order was all wrong," she said in a loud whisper.

"He's going to be so upset. We will be out of rotini, mushrooms, and even sugar by this weekend. All three were missed on the truck," the woman continued. "What should we do?"

Josie walked toward the kitchen with the woman in tow, "James will be back Friday. He'll fix it then."

I stopped drinking and set my glass down on the bar. James. My dream came back to me from the night before. But before my mind could distinguish dream and realty the older women spoke, "Yeah, go ahead make his red hair turn gray even faster."

A second later I hit the floor.

CHAPTER 80

A man that had been sitting beside me was now looking over me when I opened my eyes. He kept asking if I was okay. I wasn't sure why he was repeating himself or why I was laying on the floor.

I sat up and looked around.

I had to get out of there. I was embarrassed and confused. Before anyone else could come to my aid I was out the door.

I didn't stop running until I was waiting for the elevator in the hotel lobby. I saw my reflection in the doors before they opened. I was pale and sweating. My stomach was rolling and my head throbbed. No wonder I fainted. I was coming down with the same bug Laura and Jamie had.

When I got to the room I checked on the two patients and made sure both had water and then laid down beside Jamie and put my arm around her and watched her drift back off to sleep.

I thought about what happened at the restaurant. The stares. The whispers. The missing items from the shipment. James.

It couldn't be the same person. There had to be thousands of men named James in this world that had red hair.

It was such a coincidence though. I had the dream the night before. It was so familiar to me. I felt like it was real. Then I remembered something from that first night that we ate there. Even the chips they give you to eat while you wait are similar to the ones he made for me that night years ago, and he mentioned Houston a long time ago, didn't he?

I had to know the truth.

They said he would be back on Friday. I would be there that day to see the truth for myself.

CHAPTER 81

There were many events that have changed or shaped my life but three of the biggest have happened to me in the last five years. The first was meeting James, the second was Jamie, and the last occurred five minutes after walking into the estate attorney's office.

"Thank you both for coming in today," Mr. Copeland said, looking over the top of his reading glasses. He had just shook our hands while staying seated and was finishing up a phone call.

Laura and I didn't talk but both were probably wondering the same thing, "Why are we here?"

He hung up and proceeded to answer that exact question, "You're probably wondering why I've asked you to stay these few days past the funeral."

We nodded in unison. Jamie just held on to my arm. She had not liked the security guard in the lobby and had yet to let go of me.

"Your dad wanted you here. At least his will read that way," he said.

I slowly turned and looked at Laura with utter surprise. She looked the same but her jaw had dropped.

"Our dad? Paul Blackwell? The man who left us two decades ago? Who never returned, even for our mom's funeral?" I asked. Laura still sat with her mouth open.

"Well I don't know what kind of man he was, or why he did… or didn't do the things he should have, but I do know his will. I helped him write it and now I'm here to share it with you," Mr. Copeland said matter-of-factly.

"What about Lori Ann? Shouldn't she be here?" Laura finally spoke.

He looked down at the papers in front of him and then to Laura again over the top rim of his glasses, "Actually, no. She's not in the will and she is very much aware of it."

"Okay, well go on. Tell us what it says. Do I get the garden hose and bird feeder and Laura gets his old collection of VHS tapes and bonus tape rewinder?" I asked sarcastically. Laura kicked my left shin with the heel of her shoe. "What? You were thinking the same thing."

"Well I hate to tell you but hoses and movies weren't mentioned in the will."

"Darn," I whispered while the attorney shuffled through the file.

Finally, pulling out a colorful spreadsheet he continued, "It does say however that each of you is entitled to half of all assets - 50/50 he had said. We will start with the largest. Your father, as you obviously didn't know, was very well-off. He moved here and immediately became involved in the oil industry. It's what we're known for down here."

I listened but was stuck back at the words "well off" and of course I knew about the oil industry…pipelines…it has been haunting me for years.

"…he did well, *very* well," he stressed. "At the time of his death his savings, CD's and stocks and bonds were valued at just under 4.75 million dollars. He also had a special account set up that covered any outstanding debts, including sadly, his burial. Now, after finances we move on to real estate. This includes both his residential home and lakefront cabin, both located within the county…"

His voice drifted off. My mouth had long ago gaped open like Laura's had been but now the chair was leaning sideways and it took me a few seconds to realize that it wasn't the chair, it was me; and I was slowly falling to the floor.

Before I made it completely to the ground I sat upright but my mouth remained open. Jamie tried to close it and laughed about me being a puppet.

We signed the paperwork in silence, and went through the motions when Mr. Copeland asked questions or prodded for more information.

Thankfully, Jamie talked enough for all of us on the ride back to the hotel. She mentioned being hungry and before we could even think about anywhere else I turned into our familiar place for food, Erin Go Bragh's.

CHAPTER 82

I was nervous and scared as I opened the door to the restaurant. After passing out on their floor I was embarrassed to go back there as well. My main reason for being there today though was to curb my nagging curiosity.

"Are you better?" Josie asked as she saw me walk through the door. "When you pass…"

"I'm fine," I cut her off. Laura and Jamie didn't know what happened the other day and I didn't want to explain it now. "I think we were all cursed with the stomach bug." As I talked I scanned the room. Where was he?

We were seated at a booth at the back corner. Half the restaurant, including the bar and kitchen weren't included in our view which caused my anxiety to elevate to the ceiling.

There was still no sign of James while eating dinner. I found myself picking through my salad and ignoring conversation Laura was trying to make with me.

After the server cleared our empty plates I excused myself to find the bathroom and told Jamie and Laura that I'd meet them in the car.

I couldn't handle the suspense anymore. I needed to find out the truth, and I needed the answer right now, even if that included walking into the kitchen.

Just as I made it to the bar area I felt a hand on my arm.

"I knew I recognized you," Josie said.

"What are you talking about?" I asked confused.

"Come here." She led me to the counter and pulled something off the wall beside the register. "You're the girl from the picture."

Before I could ask what picture she was talking about Josie shoved the photograph in front of my face. The corners were slightly bent and there was a dusty film on the front but I immediately recognized the scene. It was from the day Vince took pictures at Joey's. I was smelling the rose that James game me. I looked young and happy. My heart began to race. How could anyone else have this picture? This was no longer a coincidence. I had my answer.

"Who gave that to you?" I asked, feeling my throat go dry. I thought I might pass out again.

"Well, Mr. Murphy of course. He kept it hanging up here by the register… wouldn't let anyone touch it. How do you know him?"

"James? It's his picture?" I barely spoke the questions.

"Yeah. This is his restaurant, you know," she started to laugh but stopped when she saw the surprise and shock on my face. "You didn't know. Oh my…"

The walls began to close in again and I made myself sit on the stool, this time holding on tightly to the bar in case I blacked out again. I stared at the picture for what felt like hours. When I finally forced myself to blink I looked up, tears brimming my eyes, and saw the real-life version of the man from my dream, my past standing before me.

It was James. He was beautiful.

I made myself breathe and then as I smiled I felt a warm tear crawl down my face and drop from my chin. I blindly wiped it and waited for my brain to tell me what to do next. All I could hear was my heart beating in my ears but I didn't have to wait long for the answer on what to do next.

James was by my side in seconds.

"You!" he exclaimed, looking into my eyes and smiling his perfect smile.

"You too," I said warily, melting into his arms.

He hugged me long and hard, taking my breath from my lungs.

We didn't say anything to each other, just looked into each other's eyes. Finally, I spoke the one question I've wanted to ask him since he left town that day "Where did you go?"

He didn't answer he just sighed deeply and replied. "I have a lot to talk to you about," he said. "Can you stay for a while?"

I thought of Laura and Jamie in the car, "I... I can't. Wait! Not that I don't want to... I'll come back in a little while. You will be here, right?"

"Of course. I'll actually be at that table right there. I promise," he said, pointing at the one table in the entire place that was secluded from others. It reminded me of the one from that night of our first date, when we ate on the riverside in our own private terrace.

As if reading my mind, he nodded. "I promise," he repeated.

CHAPTER 83

"Gosh, girl! Either you just saw a ghost or you're getting the flu. You're as white as a sheet!" Laura exclaimed from out the driver's window.

"You were right the first time," I gasped, not realizing I had been holding my breath.

She furrowed her brows and shook her head to let me know she didn't understand.

"I'll explain in a little while," I said, sliding into the passenger side.

To say I had a thousand thoughts running through my head would be an understatement. I didn't know where to begin in order to sort through everything. Rewinding I simply focused on James and his warm smile.

How did I not know he was right beside me this whole week, that he owned the restaurant where we ate so many meals? Then I remembered the chips the waitress had brought to our table just a few minutes ago and the last time we were there. They were so familiar to me because they were the same ones that James brought me when working at Joey's. I should have remembered that. I should have known where I had them before.

"Hey! Dazed and Confused. We're back," Laura said. "What's wrong with you, sis?"

When we got back in the room Laura said she was going to call her airline to arrange for flights out the next day in possible.

"No! I can't leave now!" I practically yelled causing both Jamie and Laura to jumped and stare with wide eyes.

She turned on a cartoon for Jamie and pulled me roughly into the bathroom, "Ok, you've got to tell me what has gotten into you.

What happened in the fifteen minutes you were in the restaurant while we were in the car?"

I flipped down the toilet seat and pointed, "You might need to sit down for this."

I then reminded her of the man who changed my life five years before. I explained that Jamie's dad was in that restaurant and that he was waiting for me to come back. "I don't know what to say, what to do. I'm so stunned and confused, and happy. I'm an emotional wreck. I can't stop the spinning wheel of feelings in order to BE just one thing," I explained.

"Wow...wow...I am just as shocked as you are. What a small world... what a freakin' small world we live in," she said, now grinning.

"I need to go to him. I need to find out what happened, why he never came back, or even called," I continued, and then whispered "... I need to tell him about Jamie."

"Yes, you do... and you need to go now while he's waiting. Jamie and I will hang out, maybe go down to the pool for a while. Don't worry about us," she said, and then as if remembering what started our bathroom discussion explained that we'd worry about the travel details later.

I hugged her as she sat on the toilet lid and went to kiss Jamie good-bye, "I have to talk to someone. I'll be back soon, baby."

I didn't make it to the door before the tears started. By the end of the hall I was a blubbering mess. I sat on the chair that faced Erin Go Bragh's and stared out the window.

"That someone I need to talk to, baby girl, is your daddy... And I'm scared to death," I whispered to myself before getting the nerve to clean my face and start the trek back across the street.

CHAPTER 84

My heart was racing and beating so forcefully that my chest wall felt like it would erupt. I was more excited than nervous, and I was practically in a run when I hit the parking lot. More cars had arrived showing the dinner rush had started, and I momentarily felt bad for taking James away when the restaurant probably needed him.

It was time for me to be selfish. I deserved a few minutes after everything I've gone through.

Quickly passing the hostess stand I left the young girl waiting with a confused smile and half greeting on her lips.

Immediately I spotted the table in the corner that James had shown me. I walked cautiously over and straining my neck looked around the wall only to see an empty seat.

My heart sank and I grabbed the table to steady myself. He wasn't there and he promised that he would be. I began to feel the pain of him leaving again and as warm tears began to well in my eyes I turned around only to see James greet me with open arms.

"What's wrong?" he asked, holding onto my arms and staring into my eyes.

"You weren't here. I thought I either imagined it or you left again," I glanced down at the last thought.

"I'm so sorry. I had a dumpster emergency…long story," he chuckled.

His laugh was like music. I smiled and slid into the booth seat.

Even though the booth was a half-circle James kept his distance by sitting across from me. I could tell he was sorry, not only for scaring me seconds before but also for leaving years ago. Time and the stress made him more rugged but even more handsome than he was before.

I couldn't help but blush.

James noticed and smiled his cock-eyed smile. "Before we start talking I want to let you know that I took the liberty to order drinks. They should be here in a little while."

"Okay." He knew I wanted to hear his excuse for leaving and not keeping in touch.

"Let me begin by apologizing a thousand times over. In fact, I'll probably say it so many times you'll get sick of hearing it." He paused and gathered his thoughts and then continued.

"My company sent me to another site… you knew that part though… but from there I began a downward spiral, my life became a series of bad misfortunes. I walked into the biggest mess of my life. The site supervisor that was there was behind schedule, short-staffed, and missing specific permits. It took me two weeks to get back on track.

"I worked fourteen to sixteen hours a day. It was ridiculous. Then, on a Tuesday afternoon I got a call I'll never forget. My step-dad had a massive heart attack. He wasn't doing well and they weren't going to let me leave. I was so tired of them taking advantage of me and not allowing anything in return so I left… that night… never said a word… and just drove all night to the hospital.

"I'm glad I did. He slipped into a coma and died three hours after I got to say goodbye."

I took his hand in silence, not noticing that the drinks had arrived. He ordered my favorite. I knew he would.

He covered my hand with his and continued, "My mom took it hard. In fact, she refused to leave the house for months. The restaurant suffered. This place was my stepfather's creation, his sweat and tears. He practically lived here and the day he died was the day this place started to struggle. I couldn't let it die with him though. I stepped in, took it over and brought it back to life. It took a while but we've recovered."

"Your pipe dream," I whispered.

"What did you say?" he asked.

"I…I said your pipe dream--owning your own restaurant. You did it," I said.

"Yeah, unfortunately it wasn't quite the circumstances I had in mind."

"I wish I would have known all this was going on with you. And how is your mom?" I asked.

He sighed deeply, "Aged twenty years, but much better. She still bakes the desserts but she doesn't like to stay here too long. And I don't need her working as hard as she once did."

"And I wish you did know what was going on. I wish I would have told you...if nothing more to be my support. I needed it and didn't know it until I had jumped in with both feet."

I sat there and stared at him trying to take in everything he told me. It made me think about him in a different light, almost feeling sorry that I ever thought anything bad of him after he left.

"What about you? Gosh, it's been five years. I'm so sorry... again... and again...You've had to have something exciting happen in that amount of time?"

I thought about Jamie but knew it was too soon to say anything. I began by telling him about school and thanked him for allowing me the opportunity to go. "I was mad at first. You had left me paid tuition for college but at the time I would have traded it in a heartbeat to have you back."

He stroked my hand but didn't comment. So I continued, "Then I realized it was your gift to me and I had to accept it. So, I graduated with my degree in Hotel and Restaurant Management. I left Joey's that same year and took a management job in the city at an upper-class place. I've been there ever since. You would like it. I've added a lot of my flavor and style to it."

"You were always a good cook," he said.

"And you, too. I've eaten here enough times to be able to recognize you in the food." I laughed.

CHAPTER 85

We laughed and drank, remembering the time we had together and filling in blanks on what went on during the five years we were apart.

As I talked I purposely forgot one important event. Jamie. I didn't know why I couldn't tell him. It didn't feel like the right moment. In a way I felt like telling him might spoil the high I was on if he took the news the wrong way.

"So, I guess the most important question I have for you is what the heck brought you to Texas?"

I was so lost in memories that I forgot about Dad. James had known my estranged, non-relationship status I held with my father. It was unbelievable to me that we were even called to be given the news of his passing.

In addition to that, and Lori-Ann, and the lawyer, I realized that this conversation may take longer that the time James could give.

"That's actually a very long conversation. I know we've already been talking for over two hours. I'm sure you have other..." I started to say but James cut me off.

"Holy cow. It's been that long. I need to relieve Molly to pick up her boys from the sitter," he said, letting go of my hands and standing up.

"Yeah, I should go too. I just wish I didn't have to," I was talking about going back to Pennsylvania.

"Are you free for breakfast tomorrow morning? I would like to continue this conversation," he asked.

I nodded, completely ignoring the fact that I was to leave. It didn't matter anyway. I knew I couldn't go home yet. Unlike when he left and his situation there was nothing keeping me from staying here.

The hug he gave me jumpstarted my heart all over again. Adrenaline pumped through my body and warmth surrounded me.

I held on as long as he allowed only letting go when he finally pulled away from me.

"Tomorrow, I'll pick you up out front of the hotel. I won't be late. No matter what disaster might happen between now and then."

I walked away but could feel him staring at me as I left. This time I smiled his famous cock-eyed smile.

CHAPTER 86

I busted through the room like I was on fire again making my two favorite girls jump out of their skin.

"Mommy, are you okay?" Jamie asked looking up from the picture book she was pretending to read.

"Yes, Mommy's great," smiling a wide smile and noticeable out of breath from running back.

Once again Laura pulled me into the bathroom. This was beginning to be a ridiculous trend. "Spill it, sister," she said.

I told her everything we talked about and described the sparks of his tender hands as he rubbed and held mine. I was reliving the moments as I retold every detail. By the end of the story Laura was as lost in thought as I was.

"We're having breakfast tomorrow. I'm not sure where but he's picking me up here," I finished.

"What about going home? Our flight is scheduled to leave by noon. Do I need to cancel?" she asked.

"Sis, I can't go. Not now. I don't know how I'll handle work or what I need to do but my life has been so tumbled around right now. The only thing I know for sure is that I can't leave here without tying up these loose ends."

"That's what I was hoping to hear," she said and I looked at her like she had a third eye on her forehead.

"*Our* plane will be leaving at ten fifty tomorrow morning," she motioned to herself and Jamie. "Your ticket is on hold until further notice."

"I don't understand."

"I thought I'd take an extended vacation and visit Gram and Pap, take Jamie home, and spend some time at the old stomping grounds. You take your time here and let me know when you're ready and I'll call the airline and get your ticket at that time. No rush. How's that sound?"

"Oh Laura!" I jumped into her arms and hugged her tightly. "I love you so much. Thank you for everything you've done for me… for us."

"Yeah, yeah, you know what they say about paybacks," she giggled.

I jumped into the bed beside Jamie and squeezed her tightly, "I love you so much pumpkin. I can't hug you enough."

"Don't! You're gonna break me!" Jamie squealed.

"I'd never break you. Laura and I need to tell you something. First, are you ready to go back home, back to school and to see Gram and Pap?"

She nodded and smiled lighting up her face.

"Aunt Laura's taking you home while Mommy stays here to work on some things, okay? But I'll be home as soon as I can and I'll talk to you every day."

She stuck out her pinky and I knew immediately what that meant. I grabbed it with mine and said, "I purple, blue and pinky swear, here there and everywhere, with a wooly bully Polar bear."

CHAPTER 87

L aura and Jamie left for the airport in a cab at eight thirty that morning. In the thirty minutes I had left to wait until James arrived I thought of twenty-six questions to ask him. I know because I wrote them down on the hotel-provided stationary pad.

As I was doodling flowers and squiggles in the margin of the paper my phone shrilled me back to reality. It was on the clock and I picked up expecting James' voice. It was instead Connie from the front desk, "Good Morning, miss. There is a very nice and handsome man waiting here for you in the lobby."

"Thank you," I said, and I hung up quickly grabbing my purse and room key.

When the elevator doors opened it took me a minute to find James. He was off to the left staring at the signature of artwork on the far wall.

"Good morning," I said when I closed my distance to him.

He turned around and handed me a single lily. "It is a good morning, isn't it?"

Once again, he knew me so well. It was the lilies I told him to order for his mom five years before. I had made the suggestion because they were my favorite flower.

He knew that then. He remembered it now.

James ushered me to his car. He had a luxury sports utility vehicle, rugged on the outside but fine leather and wood grain beauty inside – reminded me of how I would describe James, himself. I guess I shouldn't have expected anything different. I knew him well enough.

Waiting inside the vehicle was a large arrangement of flowers, mostly made up of lilies. I stood with my mouth agape and gasped at the sight. It was beautiful and completely unexpected. The single flower was surprise enough but this was astonishing.

James simply chuckled under his breath and helped me in before going around to the driver's side.

"You aren't opposed to going to my house, are you?" he asked.

I could feel myself blush but answered with a simple, "No."

"Good because breakfast is waiting there," he said. "It's about ten minutes away but you're more than welcome to tell me more until we get there."

"Actually, last night you mentioned that the most important question was what I was doing here in Texas... In fact, I think the biggest question is, why didn't you call me when you left? I mean, I had no idea where you went or where you lived. I searched everywhere for you. It was like you disappeared and it honestly felt like that's what you wanted." I waited.

He took in a deep breath as if knowing this question would come, "Actually, I did call. A few times. I called Joey's and some young Italian guy said you were on a date and weren't working."

I knew that was Anthony, Joey's nephew, who would have been working the bar that night. Instead of saying anything though I waited for him to continue.

"The second time I called and, who I think may have been Mickey answered and said you were in the back but that he'd tell you to call back. He called me Evan. There may have been a time or two after that I tried you at Joey's again.

"I also called your house and there was no answer. I told myself that you moved on and promised I would never call back, no matter how tempted I was. I began to feel like a stalker. How is Evan?"

I remembered Evan told me he had told him I moved on. I shouldn't have been but I was shocked. Hot tears welled in my eyes, and I instantly became upset. I looked for anyone and everything to blame. Why didn't someone tell me, or why didn't I pick up the phone at least one of those times? I blinked back the tears and stared out the front window as James drove. I couldn't talk, just shook my head in response.

"I want you to know I tried. I never forgot about you. And honestly,

I've never truly been happy. Even if you moved on, I couldn't," he said.

"I'm so sorry… sorry for all of it. I'm sorry I didn't get to talk to you, to take your call. And no, I didn't move on. I tried. There was nothing that gave me happiness though. It was like a child who lost a cat. That may be a silly animal to some but it was all that child could think of. All that would be in that kid's heart until it came home. Do you understand what I'm saying or is it just as silly?" I asked, embarrassed for how the situation went but upset for not being aware of any of it.

"Well, actually, I know exactly what you mean – literally and fig-uratively," he said, putting the car in park on the street in front of a cute two-story brick house. "And there's no need to worry anymore, I'm home."

CHAPTER 88

James' house was very organized with décor and furniture in coordinating neutral colors. A Chocolate Labrador met us at the entryway. His coloring matched the rest of the accessories in the room, which made me smile.

Everything was in place and even the smell of the house was appropriate. I was a little surprised by how neat he kept the place.

"This is the living room on the left and dining on the right, of course," he said, beginning his narrative for the tour he was taking me on.

Walking through the dining room he continued, "And this is my favorite room, the kitchen. I'll be found here most of my waking hours."

On the final leg of the tour James quickly showed me around the upstairs, only pausing briefly by the doorway of his bedroom. I tried not to blush but could feel my cheeks grow red.

"Okay, so let's go downstairs and I'll finish breakfast." He quickly directed me back downstairs.

He motioned for me to sit on a stool at the bar in the kitchen. "Coffee's done. Would you like a cup?"

"Of course. You know I must have coffee in the mornings," I said.

Then, as if someone pressed a fast forward button on him he quickly but smoothly began to throw breakfast together. He went from scrabbling eggs to sliding bacon into the oven to crisp, back to stirring batter for what looked like blueberry pancakes. He would pour batter onto the griddle with his right hand while stirring the skillet of eggs with his left.

I sat and sipped my coffee watching in amazement. Finally, I asked him to tell me more about his house and the restaurant. I didn't want to press him for information but I felt left out not being allowed to help with the cooking.

Not skipping a beat, he began talking about his Texas life, "Actually, the only thing I've done since taking over the restaurant was just that, working at the restaurant. If I'm not there I'm running errands or picking up shipments for the kitchen, or I'm crashed here, probably still in my shoes and face down on the couch."

"I feel your pain," I said. "Running a restaurant is very hard work. I'm just the manager and was only the bartender at Joeys but could see how it can age a person."

He stopped mid stir and flip. "Wait. Are you saying I'm old now?"

I laughed and shook my head violently, "Never. You look the same as you did five years ago… well, maybe better. You're cleaner now."

It was James' turn to laugh. He turned around and went back to work. That was when I noticed a picture on the dining room hutch of a brunette and James with their arms around each other. My adrenaline immediately coursed through my veins and my heart went from excited to breaking.

Why was I acting like this? It was a terrible feeling of jealousy, and there was no reason to have it. James and I weren't together and didn't even know each other was even still alive in the last five years.

I was staring at the hutch when James turned around with two plates in his hand.

"What's wrong?" he asked, setting them down.

"Oh, nothing. I must still be tired." I tried to cover up with the only excuse I could pull out of thin air.

He looked over and noticed what I had seen. "Ahh, that's a good picture, huh? That's Ashley. She's my wife."

CHAPTER 89

I couldn't even think of words let alone speak any. I just sat there and looked as if a ghost just walked past.

"Man, you look like you just saw a ghost?" He laughed. "Let me clarify so you calm down. Ashley and I were married, but only Tuesdays through Saturday during August of 1998. We were in a community play together…Mr. and Mrs. Stanley Bellshire. Suckered to do it by the women at work I couldn't say no."

Finally I blinked and then forced a smile. "That sounds like fun."

"It actually was a lot of fun. I surprised myself with a little bit of talent, too," he said, sitting on the stool beside me. "I am so glad to see you again."

This time I didn't hide the blush that washed over my face. I barely picked at my food but made sure he understood it was nothing to do with his cooking. "I shouldn't be nervous but it's been so long that I just can't get used to the fact that you and I are sitting here… together… in your house."

"Okay, well let's go sit in the living room then and get used to one another."

I followed him to the L-shaped sofa and put one leg under me and plopped down with my coffee. "I actually have something I wanted to talk to you about."

There were two things I knew I couldn't mention yet. One of them was Jamie. The other was the inheritance. But he had wanted to know what brought me to Texas so I told him about how my father passed away and his girlfriend called us out of the blue to invite us to the funeral.

"That's crazy. Was she a good person?"

214

"Actually, she was so much nicer, and well… more normal than I ever thought she could be. It made me sad to know that the call came too late. I should have gotten the call months or years earlier so I could have seen him when he was alive.

I can't believe our hotel was right beside your restaurant. That was very ironic. Almost, fate-like."

"Yeah, it was certainly fate-like," he said, repeating my made-up word. "But you said, 'our hotel' was your sister with you? Is she still here? I wish I could meet her."

I felt my heart rate increase again as I knew what I was about to say would be a string of lies, "She actually had to leave and go back to work. I told her I'd stay here and work out the burial and will with the lawyer."

"Oh, and I thought it was to spend time with me," James said and chuckled.

If he only knew.

CHAPTER 90

After breakfast James offered to show me around other parts of the city. He said the first stop was to meet someone. I was surprised that he wanted to introduce me to anyone but he seemed excited and practically drug me by the arm into a tall high rise off a busy Houston street.

We rode in silence to the 36th floor. The only sounds I heard was the hushed breathing of James from racing through the lobby and the static elevator music version of an old Rod Stewart song.

When the doors opened a well-lit reception area appeared with a young woman talking on the phone. She waved at James and nodded as if answering an unspoken question.

He turned to the right and walked swiftly to the end of a bright hallway.

A man was turned looking out the window behind the desk and he was patting his head with his left hand while holding the telephone receiver to his ear with the right. He wasn't talking and the sound of us entering his office made him turn around and immediately drop the phone back into the cradle. I hoped there was nobody on the other end.

"Hey bro... what are you doing down here today?" the man exclaimed.

I immediately knew who this was, simply from the facial features and similar hair.

"Annie, this is my brother Eric. Eric... This is Annie." The way he introduced me made me sound like a star.

Eric immediately jumped up and extended his hand across the desk. His chair flew into the filing cabinet behind him.

"*The* Annie? Wow, it's so nice to finally meet you. I told you that you're a fool, James. How the heck did you find her?"

I simply shook his hand but kept an obvious look of confusion on my face. "You're kind of famous around here, and she found me," James explained. "See, if we bet money I would have lost. They all said you'd come back in my life. I unfortunately lost hope in fate."

"Well, it's me. I'm Annie, and I never give up hope in fate," I said, smiling shyly.

"So, what are you two doing today?"

"Visiting the city. In fact, coming here was the first thing on my list."

"And I'm so glad you did. I do need to run though. Class starts in ten minutes," Eric said, lifting a briefcase onto his desk.

"Eric is the director of a culinary institute. He might be younger but he certainly taught me a lot in the kitchen," James said.

Eric ushered us toward the door and just as I crossed the threshold I overheard him whisper to James, "Did you talk to the bank yet?"

I heard James reply, "Yeah, unfortunately I did. I'll tell you about it later. I'll call you this evening."

I put that brief conversation in the back of my mind. I didn't want to pry but it made me wonder what it all meant.

CHAPTER 91

We rode in silence down the city streets of Houston. He could tell I was thinking something and asked what was on my mind. "Just wondering where we're headed to next," I lied.

"Well, I'm glad you asked. See, I need to know which way to go up here at the next stoplight. Pick left for walking, right for riding. Either way you win because we're going both ways before the day's over," he said.

I thought about the decision for a few seconds before answering him. "Ok, let's walk. Go left."

He dropped me off in front of a building with a long set of front steps but no signs. As he parked the vehicle I quickly ascended the steps. A door embedded in dark glass met me at the top. There were simple letters "HCP". I waited by the door and kept my eyes on the road wishing he'd hurry back from parking.

Surprisingly I heard his lovely voice behind me, "Glad of you to join me, my lady."

I followed his beckoning hand inside and was greeted with a rush of cold air conditioning.

The entryway was dark and I could see light flooding from the left and right hallways. "Where are we?" I asked.

"This is the Houston Center for Photography," he answered, grabbing my hand and guiding me down the right hallway.

I never knew he was any kind of art fanatic, and certainly not the photography or 'museumy' kind of guy.

Before I could ask him why we were here he pointed at a picture on the wall. I instantly knew it was him. He was sitting on a bench with a woman with graying hair. They were facing the opposite direction and you could see a blurry lake in the background. The woman had her head laid on James shoulder and the title of the picture was 'Role reversal'.

"Me and my mom," he said softly, "Most people will see this picture but never know the reasoning behind why the photo was taken. My stepdad took this picture right before I left for the pipeline trip to Pennsylvania. When we were sitting on the bench my stepdad took it because there was a similar one we had at the house where I was laying my head on my mom's shoulder on the same bench. I come here a lot to think about those times. I also came here to think about you, too."

I squeezed his hand tighter and without thinking about it I automatically laid my head on his shoulder and we stared at the picture together.

I thought back to the first time I saw James. He was beautiful to me. Some would probably think he was a rough rider from out of town and I could only see a gentle lover. It was at this moment that my instinct was confirmed. He could have taken me anywhere or even nowhere for that matter but chose to show this moment of his life to me.

He brought me back to the present by telling me it was time to move on to the next place.

"If it's okay with you... and I don't want to sound like I'm not having fun. I am. I enjoy everything we're doing...together. But can we find time to just talk. I feel like we're moving in fast forward and I need to just... just step back," I said.

"Yes, where we're going next we have plenty of time to do just that."

"Perfect."

We again rode in silence to the next destination. It was funny how the car affected our conversations. I knew I had a million thoughts running through my head. I assumed the same was happening to James as well.

As he pulled into the parking lot of a marina I was looking around for signs of the next plan. I didn't hear him when he first asked, "When do you meet with the lawyer?"

He waited until I was once again in the safety of his hand. "You mentioned needing to see the lawyer about your father's estate. When is your appointment?"

Without looking at him I simply said two words that were the beginning of a life changing conversation, "About that…"

CHAPTER 92

The next stop of our journey together around the Houston area took us to the historical side of town. His plan was to show me the 'other side of the tracks' so he said. Instead I did most of the talking.

As we sat side by side in the cart of an electric rickshaw I told James how a week ago I still didn't even know where my father was living, nor did I know if he was even alive. And then, only days later my sister and I learn that my father had money and now my sister and I have become owners of the small fortune.

When I finished I realized that I probably had said too much. It was a very personal event that happened to me but I felt more comfortable talking to James than anyone else I've ever known in my life, and that included my sister, mom, or even grandparents.

I gently smiled and waited for him to say something.

Finally, he spoke. "That's absolutely wonderful news Annie. I mean, there is nobody that I know that deserves it more."

"Thank you. I know it's hard to admit it, but it really will help. I mean, I could actually open the restaurant that I've always dreamed about… not have to work for the 'man'. Things could be just like I want them," I explained.

"Yeah, it's easier when there is money involved," he said with a sad tone.

I looked around at the tree lined streets. It was a beautiful place but I realized I missed home. I had seen Jamie hours before but it was like I left her when I got on the plane to fly here.

When we were both silent for a few moments I asked if he was okay.

He nodded and I didn't pursue. I didn't have to. He offered a detailed reply and in doing so answered the question on how his conversation ended with his brother.

"When my step-dad died and Mom tried to take over she decided the only way to keep the business going strong would be to get a second mortgage and renovate, making the place bigger and in turn hiring more staff, more utilities… well, you know… everything else that came with more space. Then, with her stepping down and the bills coming due, we got behind and have been trying to play catch up ever since. Unfortunately, it's not working very well."

He continued without even taking a breath, "I mean, I don't want to sell. I will of course… if I have to. Eric's always mentioned coming to help out but with the school now, he just can't do it. I really don't want to let it go… it's been in the family you know? But we have good news. I talked with the manager at the bank. I think we have a plan to make it work."

When he finished he smiled, either to make sure I didn't worry, or to make himself stronger. I returned his smile.

And this is when I knew I could never go home without him, or without at least knowing I'd see him again.

His phone interrupted us. "Hello," he said impatiently, not wanting to be bothered.

His side of the conversation sounded like this, "No. No, I wasn't told that. Well, why wasn't it included? I mean I was JUST in Dallas. You've got to be kidding. What did he say? Really? We can't wait for it to be delivered Monday. The dinner is scheduled for Saturday night. That's fine. No. Tell him when he calls back that he'll be seeing my smiling face in a few hours."

Then, as he hung up he turned to me, "What do you think about making the next stop on our date Dallas?"

CHAPTER 93

I should have said no. I wanted to say no. But when I opened my mouth the only word that my brain had floating around was the same that came from my mouth, "Yes."

He took a deep breath, "Good. Well let's get your luggage from the hotel. They forgot the zinfandel from the wine order.... Got the merlot, but the host of the party only drinks a unique kind of zinfandel. If I knew I needed a special bottle I would have checked before I left the winery."

I tried to tame the butterflies that flapped against my stomach walls as we road quickly back to the hotel. When he pulled up to the door I told him I'd be right back. I had already packed my things knowing my fairy tale would soon come to an end.

Connie wasn't working today but the young man that was in her place seemed just as disappointed to see me checking out. I thanked them for a great stay and was quickly out in the parking lot.

James had the trunk open and the engine was still running. I jumped in and within minutes we were on the highway to Dallas. He had been on the phone when I got in the car and was still talking ten minutes later. I could tell the person on the other end of the phone was upset. Even though he tried to hide his comments I understood that the caller was a bank representative and the news he gave wasn't what James was expecting.

When he hung up he drove in silence. The anger didn't show on his face and in fact, he smiled at me. He simply didn't say anything, just reached over and gripped my hand holding it tightly.

I knew it would be a long ride if he didn't talk so I asked what was wrong.

He simply replied, "The bank can't help me. In order to get an equity loan, I'd need equity…which we don't have. I can't refinance, and they said my assets are not enough to cover any type of other loan. I'm stuck. I don't want to sell but if we can't get the bank to help us I don't have a choice."

"What does your brother say?" I asked.

He shifted into the fast lane and said, "Honestly, I don't think he cares. He's moved on with his school and I thought he'd be the one to take over the family business. He's the restaurant person, not me. I'm still going to call him though…"

"Yeah, but I remember the dream you told me about years ago. I know you wouldn't want to throw in the towel. Unfortunately though, dreams are sometimes hard to obtain, and that includes roadblocks such as this."

We talked the entire way to Dallas. It was so comfortable being in the car with him. When we pulled into the winery he opened my door and took my hand. It was unspoken but I knew we were as together as in the past.

He spoke to the manager in the office as I roamed the shop picking up cheeses, candles, and my own bottle of wine. I might as well take advantage of the trip.

As we paid he asked the question even though he knew before that we would have to stay. "So, do you think we should find a place to stay or head home and drive through the night?"

I wanted to laugh wondering if he remembered mentioning getting my luggage before we left, "Let's find a hotel. I'm actually exhausted from having to get up early to go to the airport."

"That's what I was hoping you'd say."

CHAPTER 94

My butterflies returned. I was embarrassed, excited, and undeniably anxious. I wanted so badly to just be in his arms again. But so many changes happened within the last five years, including the addition of a child, our child. It can't be easy. We couldn't just fall back into each other's lives like before. I had to fight the feelings I was beginning to get again.

James respected my privacy. He paid for one night but for two rooms. As fate would have it though our rooms were not only side by side but they were also adjoining.

"Just perfect," I said to myself as I sat down on the bed and faced the doorway to his room. "How am I to make this easier on myself when I'm sleeping twenty feet away?"

I threw myself backward and lay flat on the perfect duvet cover. I hoped to close my eyes and just fall asleep and not worry about dealing with this tonight. Not two minutes later though the phone next to me shrilled me back to reality.

I simply reached over and put the receiver to my ear. "Yes?"

"Hey, wanna order Chinese with me?" James asked.

"Sure."

I hung up the phone and then walked to the connecting door and unlocked my side knocking on his for entry.

"Can I help you?" He laughed as he opened the door.

"Avon calling!" I said, and laughed, too.

He took down my order and then called the first Chinese restaurant listed in the phone book that delivered. While we waited the eighteen minutes we were told we sat at the table and paged through the phone book calling out guesses as to whose name would be on what page. It was a game we first played one slow night at Joey's. Before we quit playing we would randomly point to any name in the book and that is what we would call each other for the rest of the night. Tonight, James became Tommy Valentino and I was Margret Morton.

We shared our Cashew Chicken and Mongolian Beef and ate in mostly silence. We would smile when catching the other staring and laugh after long periods of silence. I know we were both wondering the same thing. How would this night end?

I was exhausted. As I finished eating I threw my trash away and walked toward my room. We had left the doors opened and I could see the light shining in from the end table.

"Thank you for dinner." I paused in the doorway.

"Anytime Annie Oakley," he said.

"Not Annie... Margret," I corrected.

Then, like I magnet I was drawn into his arms. I know in my mind I tried to resist but my legs wouldn't stop and before I knew it I had turned and walked back toward him. In seconds I was enveloped in his arms and he was kissing me as passionately as he did five years ago.

We simultaneously walked toward the bed, not releasing our lips and sank down as one.

While he lay over top of my body he looked into my eyes and said, "I'm so glad you're back, Margret."

"Me too, Tommy," I said and pulled him into my chest.

There was no longer a question of how the night would end.

CHAPTER 95

I woke up as the sun was rising. I listened to the birds chirp outside and their rhythm matched that of the deep breaths in my ear. I was cradled in the arms of the man I loved. I could see the light still shining from my room and I smiled, thinking of what a waste it was paying for two rooms.

I lay there staring at the brightening sun and thinking about the week I had. So much had happened in so little time that I felt like this was the first moment I had to actually begin to sort everything out. On top of everything Texas threw at me I needed to get back to Pennsylvania, to my job and to Jamie.

Jamie.

How do I explain her to him and not have it look like I was keeping her a secret? I groaned.

James stirred beside me and pulled me closer to his chest, nuzzling my neck. "Good morning," he whispered into my ear.

"I turned and smiled into his slit eyes. Sorry, it's such a beautiful and bright day, I couldn't stay asleep," I said.

"No, we need to get going anyway. I need to get back before the afternoon." He pulled himself out of bed and I stared at his naked backside as he sauntered to the bathroom.

I wrapped the sheet around myself and called out that I would be in my room. "Give me ten minutes and I'll be ready," I said.

I jumped in the shower and with my face in the spray yelped as I felt hands reach around and cup my breasts. James kissed my neck and we began another round of lovemaking. I grabbed the wall and gave into him almost falling from sheer ecstasy. A thick fog of steam filled the room and when I turned to look at James I couldn't tell if the mist was bothering him of if the tough man in front of me was crying.

"I truly missed you so much, and I'm sorry," he said, pulling me into his arms.

"Not as much as I missed you," I answered.

CHAPTER 96

I was quiet as I sat in the car on the way back to Houston. I wanted to blurt out that James had a daughter and that she was the most beautiful creation ever made. Instead I just sat in silence, scared at what might happen if I did.

When James asked what was wrong I lied and told him I was tired. It had been a long week. He understood and bought it. I even pretended to sleep in the passenger seat. Instead of closing my eyes I stared out the window at the trees as they zoomed past.

Finally, his cell phone broke the silence. But I kept still, pretending to still be asleep.

"Yes. This is he," James said to the unknown voice on the other end of the conversation.

"I understand. Yes. I'm very much aware of what is owed," he lowered his voice, but in the car, everything is shared.

He sat for a few minutes before again raising his voice.

"No, unfortunately, that isn't possible. Yes, I know. That's my mother. No, she's not on the account anymore. It's my restaurant now. I know. And yes, like I said, I understand it's just not possible to give you that much. No. It won't be good to call back in a week. Or a month. I won't have it for a while."

Then instead of saying goodbye he simply slammed the cell phone shut, and I jumped.

"Damn collection agents," he said and then added, "I'm sorry for scaring you. I know you were sleeping."

"No, it's okay. Are you okay, though? What was that about?" And as soon as I said it I was embarrassed for prying.

"Yeah, I'm fine." He sighed deeply. Then after squinting he looked at the horizon, as if thinking about what to say, he continued, "I'm still dealing with the mess of bills my mom accumulated. I'll never get caught up, and I'll honestly be lucky to stay afloat this year."

"I'm so sorry to hear that." I sincerely meant it. Pains of sorrow formed in my chest.

"I've tried. That's what I can honestly say. There was a big hole to fill, and I gave it my best. I mean I've turned that place completely around. I just think I was too late."

I reached over and held his hand. Then, we once again went back to sitting in silence. This time, both of us staring out the windshield deep in thought.

CHAPTER 97

As we pulled into the parking lot of the restaurant it was clear that my time in Houston was coming to an end. I was feeling like I was being pulled into too many directions at the same time. I didn't know where I needed to be right now. I needed to get home. I needed to be in Houston with James. I needed to get the financial situation straightened out with the estate.

I had acquired a new house, renewed a lost relationship, and found new responsibilities all within a week. As James opened his door and unloaded the supplies I stayed glued to the passenger seat, afraid to move and even more afraid of what I would say if I opened my mouth. I fought to keep from crying or worse screaming.

He looked at me through the driver's window as he walked to the back door of the restaurant. I smiled and quickly dialed Laura on the phone showing him I needed to make a call through the window. He nodded and pointed with his head letting me know where he'd be.

She didn't answer, and I left her a message telling me to call back as soon as she could. I knew she was going to be arranging my flight back home, and I promised her I'd check in to see how Jamie was doing.

If anything, the call would buy me time in private to calm down.

Even with all the time spent in the car to think I still needed more of it. I knew it was inevitable. I would have to go back home. I just now realized I couldn't do it alone.

It was then that I saw the same blue pickup truck that ran us off the road after the funeral. It was parked by the back entrance. Once again, he was so close yet so unknown to me. Could I ever let him go again?

CHAPTER 98

Twenty minutes later I was still sitting in the car. Laura had called me back, and I explained my plan to her. She told me I was crazy but agreed.

After that much time, James must have realized I wasn't coming inside and came to find me. After looking at me cautiously through the driver's window he opened the door and climbed inside.

"Um, are you coming in?" he asked with a half-smile.

I kept my lips together, smiled, and shook my head.

"Oh! Is everything okay?" His half smile faded.

This time I nodded, opening my eyes wide, but still keeping my lips sealed.

He looked at me cockeyed for a few minutes before finally asking what was going on.

I took in a deep breath and began, "I need you to listen to everything I tell you before you say a word, okay?"

This time he nodded, even though he did so suspiciously. He slowly eased into the seat beside me as if fire would rage up and consume him at any moment.

I waited before he shut the door to continue, "I have a plan...a big... no, very big plan actually. But I need you to come to Pennsylvania with me. My sister has gotten us a flight this evening. I know it's short notice. But you need to come. It's very important. I have something to tell you, well, actually a couple important things to tell you, and one very important one to show you. I trusted you to go to Dallas. Can you trust me to come to Pennsylvania?"

I expected him to laugh.

I expected him to tell me I was crazy, that there was no way he could leave the restaurant, especially with everything going on there.

But he didn't do either.

He took my hand. And he simply nodded showing his complete trust and faith in me.

2010

EPILOGUE

Waiting on the front porch for the school bus, I thought back to that day in Houston. I left...by myself. It was the longest plane ride and wait I ever painfully went through.

He didn't come.

He had said he would follow me but weeks went by. I didn't hear anything. During that time my grandfather passed away. I needed James there to cry on his shoulder, to help me with the funeral arrangements.... To finally meet his daughter.

But he wasn't there. I was so mad and overwhelmingly sad. Between all the chaos that was happening, I called his restaurant. At first they told me he wasn't available. Then, eventually the number was no longer in service.

After exhaustive nights of crying and having to make up excuses as to why my puffy eyes were always swollen I crawled into bed and prayed. I asked the Lord to help me move on. But if he had other plans to make me aware of them or give me the strength to wait. I couldn't go on anymore. I wasn't eating. I never slept. My hopes of becoming part owner of the restaurant were gone. I barely drug myself out of bed to see Jamie off to school. I would just be able to get to the couch so my work knew I was anything but reliable anymore.

The day after my prayer I woke up with a burst of energy. I made a big breakfast for me and Jamie, cleaned the house the entire day while she was in school, and as I was dialing the number to work to let them know I was back I heard a repetitive beeping outside my door. I separated the blinds with two fingers and saw it.

He was there.

Driving the biggest truck I'd ever seen, he was attempting to back it into my driveway but finally gave up and hopped down from the cab. I was in his arms in a matter of seconds.

"Good! I found the right place." He laughed.

Again I found myself crying for days, but this time with a smile on my face.

"Mommy," I heard the cutest voice bringing me back to today.

I reached down and hugged the screaming child, practically falling backward.

"Johnny, be careful," James said with Jamie's arms locked around his neck enjoying a free piggy-back ride.

John Paul was born five years ago. Timing of his birth made him a product of the visit to Houston many years ago. Yes, I was pregnant with him out of wedlock, too. If my mother was rolling in her grave from Jamie, she would have been convulsing knowing about John. In defense we didn't know he was in the oven until we were on our honeymoon. The desire to dip my toes into the sand was replaced with my head in the toilet. It became confirmed with a red plus sign on an overpriced pregnancy test from the only store on the island we could find.

Our small wedding was planned for one month after James arrived. I couldn't wait another second to be with him. I didn't want anything else keeping us apart. After a twelve-minute hug he had dropped to one knee, pulled out a ring and asked my hand in marriage. Getting his mother's ring fitted and reset was the reason he was delayed in coming to see me. I forgave him.

Those most important to me were by my side as he promised to love me forever from the bank of the river just outside the city. The sunset on the water was perfect. We each held Jamie's hand as we walked back down the aisle. The reception that followed was at Joey's of course and life was finally perfect.

With the money my father left me we reopened Erin Go Bragh's—this time in Pennsylvania. James said an Irish restaurant can work in any state. His mom was given the house that dad also willed to me. The rest of the money was put into college funds for the kids. I didn't want them worrying about their education like I did.

As I look at my family laughing and hugging each other I am so blessed. I can't thank the Lord enough for answering my prayers, giving me the strength to continue. He knew he was bringing this man back to me.

Life is good.

And I think to myself...

...*What a Wonderful World.*

ABOUT THE AUTHOR

KL Collins calls herself the *working mother's author.*

Even though she hasn't (yet) written a book on how to be a better mom, or how to incorporate your personal life into your long work day; she did follow her dream and write a novel...or two. She hopes to inspire other working moms to write, or follow their dreams wherever they lead, and not give up.

One thing that sets Collins apart from other authors is her propensity to write with 'break' chapters in mind – chapters short enough to take a bathroom break, commercial break, or smoke break away from life, each averaging two to three pages. She wants to bring reading back into the lives of busy people; to show them you can, in fact, enjoy a book and take time for yourself; and to do so with the limited and precious spare time you have.

Born and raised in a quiet Amish-surrounded community in Pennsylvania, she now resides in Tennessee with her family. In addition to being employed full time in a corporate real estate position, Collins remains passionate about her church and her writing. She jokes that her mind never shuts off. Even in the most inopportune time she's jotting down ideas for the next manuscript. Just don't tell her boss!

Also Available From

KL Collins

27 Words
The Endurants
Twice as Different

Also Available From

WordCrafts Press

Maggie's Song
    by Marcia Ware

End of Summer
    by Michael Potts

You've Got It, Baby!
    by Carmichael

Glory Revealed, Sisters of Lazarus, Book 2
    by Paula K. Parker

Home
    by Eleni McKnight

Tears of Min Brock
    by J.E. Lowder

Ill Gotten Gain
    by Ralph E. Jarrells

www.wordcrafts.net

CPSIA information can be obtained
at www.ICGtesting.com
Printed in the USA
JSHW032238260922
31028JS00006B/33

9 780999 647523